Level 13

a slacker novel

LOOK FOR MORE ACTION AND HUMOR FROM
GORDON KORMAN

THE HYPNOTISTS SERIES
The Hypnotists
Memory Maze
The Dragonfly Effect

THE SWINDLE SERIES
Swindle
Zoobreak
Framed
Showoff
Hideout
Jackpot
Unleashed
Jingle

The Titanic trilogy

The Kidnapped trilogy

The On the Run series

The Dive trilogy

The Everest trilogy

The Island trilogy

War Stories

Restart

Slacker

Whatshisface

Radio Fifth Grade

The Toilet Paper Tigers

The Chicken Doesn't Skate

This Can't Be Happening at Macdonald Hall!

GORDON KORMAN

Level 13

a slacker novel

SCHOLASTIC INC.

This book was originally published in hardcover by Scholastic Press in 2019.

ISBN 978-1-338-28621-2

10 9 8 7 6 5 4 3 2 1   20 21 22 23 24

Printed in the U.S.A.   40
This edition first printing 2020

Book design by Nina Goffi

For the Sardos:
Mike, Rosanne, Anna, and Joe

CHAPTER ONE
CAMERON BOXER

Flying in on a battle bus—it didn't get much more ill than that.

The setup: On the wide-screen TV, the map—meaning the island—ready to be invaded by fifty battle royale players, including me. The *me* part was important, since this was my live game stream. A webcam captured my every move. On the coffee table, a laptop showed exactly what my online followers would be seeing—my amazing gameplay, and in a window in the top corner, a view of me working the controller like I was born to do it. Which I was.

The far side of the stream page was reserved for viewer comments. Right now there were none, because I hadn't gone live yet. Another possible reason for that was the fact that I only had eight followers, and one of them was my own phone. Everything has to start somewhere. Top gaming streamers could have hundreds of thousands, maybe even millions of subscribers. Their every move was eagerly watched by hordes of fans all over the world.

My father always told me, "I know video games are your hobby, Cam, but they'll never be a real job." Wrong, Dad. If you had enough subscribers, you could make truckloads of cash. Besides, I always found the word *hobby* a little insulting. Gaming was a lot more than a hobby for me. It was my lifestyle. And if I could start up a successful stream now—while I was still in middle school—I might never have to get a real job.

My guidance counselor, Mr. Fan-something, said that it was important to choose a career that gave you pleasure and satisfaction. Well, that was a slam dunk for me. I'd be getting *paid* to play video games!

It would all start with the flip of a switch. My thumb reached for the button on the controller in my hands.

Ding-dong!

I ignored the doorbell. There were no doorbells on the island.

The bell sounded a second time and then a third. This was followed by loud, persistent pounding on the door.

"Somebody get that!" I shouted, before remembering that I was alone in the house.

Next, my phone began to ring. That bothered me. With my phone tied up, my follower count went down to seven.

I answered it. "What?"

"Cam—I'm at your house!" It was Jordan Toleffsen, one of Sycamore Middle School's student government types.

"Yeah, it sounds like you're about to bust the door down." We had a history of door problems at our house, so

I was kind of sensitive about it. It was mostly my fault—and the fire department's. But that was another story.

"You're *home*?" He was incredulous. "String's party started half an hour ago!"

"String knows I might not be able to make it." At least he'd figure it out when I didn't show up.

"Don't you know anything about *optics*?" *Optics* was one of Jordan's favorite political words. "You're head of the Positive Action Group. You have to be *seen* there!"

Positive Action Group. I had no one to blame but myself for that. In my own defense, I only invented the P.A.G. to make myself look like a student leader so Mom and Dad wouldn't ban me from video games. It was never supposed to become a real club.

But there was no way to tell that to the 874 kids who joined, eager to pick up garbage, walk old ladies across the street, paint the orphanage, and do all kinds of other community service.

Not that there was anything bad about community service. We helped a lot of people. I even got kind of into it toward the end. The problem was community service took up a lot of prime gaming time.

The happiest day of my life was when the principal disbanded the P.A.G. last fall. Suddenly, I had my life back, and nobody could even blame me for it. It was Dr. LaPierre's fault, not mine. It was paradise.

Then the P.A.G. got reinstated—just when my streaming career was about to take off.

Paradise lost.

"Tell String I can't get away," I told Jordan over the phone. "Better yet, don't tell him anything. There are going to be a zillion people at the party. No one will ever notice I'm not there."

"Are you nuts? *Everyone* will notice! You're Cam Boxer!"

The kids in this town—they really knew how to hurt a guy.

"Listen—" A click signified that I was getting another call. "Hang on a sec." As soon as I switched over, I could hear loud music and a lot of excited chatter.

"Cam?" I instantly identified the deep voice over the background noise. Xavier Meggett—another pagger, as P.A.G. members referred to themselves. And judging by the music, he was definitely at the party. "Where are you?" Xavier demanded. "You're coming, right?"

My heart sank. It was one thing to blow off Jordan, but *Xavier*? He was two years older than the rest of us. He got held back a couple of times because his family sent him on "trips"—code for another stretch in juvie. For him, the P.A.G. wasn't just community service; it was Community Service—the kind you got sentenced to by a judge. In Xavier's eyes, the club had straightened out his whole life.

4

"Xavier—hi! How's the party?"

"It'll be better when you get here," came his deep baritone.

Another click. "Sorry, Xavier. Gotta take this." I switched to the third call, which was from Pavel Dysan, one of my two best friends. Along with Chuck Kinsey, we made up the Awesome Threesome—or at least that's what we called ourselves on the gaming circuit.

"You'd better sit down, Cam. This is technically huge. And if you're eating anything, spit it out. You'll choke when you hear this."

The background music was a perfect match for Xavier's. I couldn't believe it. "Are you at String's party?" I challenged. "You're supposed to be watching my stream! I go live any minute!"

"You've got to reschedule, man. This is an emergency. Chuck—"

Someone cranked up the volume, drowning out Pavel's voice.

"What about Chuck?" I shouted into the phone. "Is he there with you?" Pavel and Chuck were two of my eight followers. If they were both at the party, that left only six— and one of the six was *me*. Even if my entire fan base showed up online, I'd be streaming for, at most, five people. Eight was nothing to write home about, but five was pathetic.

Obviously, I couldn't start streaming until I put in an appearance at this party.

I shut off everything and headed upstairs, shrugging into a jacket. I threw open the door and rushed outside, slamming pretty hard into Jordan and sending the two of us rolling across the lawn. Who knew the guy would still be there after I blew him off? If I'd gone out the back way, would he have still been standing on my stoop tomorrow morning?

"Sorry," I mumbled as we brushed ourselves off.

We walked the four blocks to the home of Freeland "First String" McBean, star wide receiver and flanker back of the Sycamore Middle School Seahawks.

Jordan talked nonstop every step of the way. "I want to go into politics when I grow up. That's why I joined the P.A.G. in the first place—I thought it could help me get elected student body president. But elections are all about beating the other candidate. And in the P.A.G. we learned that cooperation is what gets things done and makes the world a better place . . ."

He went on and on. The closer we got to the McBean house, the harder it was to hear him. The music was blasting through the whole neighborhood. Halfway up the front walk, he stopped, regarding me expectantly.

"What?" I asked, mystified.

"So what do you think I should do?"

I hadn't listened to a single word for the past three blocks. I remembered something about politics, but after the first couple of minutes of boringness, my mind automatically filed it under Who Cares? Part of my lifestyle was filtering out all the white noise so I could keep my focus razor-sharp on video games, where it belonged.

But Jordan looked so serious, so anxious to hear my viewpoint, that I didn't have the heart to tell him I'd tuned out. "Why would you ask me about—you know—that?"

My answer seemed to baffle him. "Because you're Cam Boxer. The P.A.G. is your baby. If anybody's got his head screwed on straight, it has to be you."

I was staring at him when the door burst open. "Cam!" String reached out his long receiver's arms, locked them around my neck, and hauled me into the house. "Hey, everybody! *Cam's here!*"

The roar of *"Cam!"* drowned out the blaring music. I was pulled through the crush of bodies, my back pounded, my hands high-fived, and my shoulders slapped. I was very nearly hugged breathless. It was a perfect example of why I hadn't wanted to come in the first place. It was nice to be loved, but not to be loved so much that you didn't have five seconds to get your streaming career off the ground. I almost started to wish people would hate me a little bit— or at least leave me alone.

String gave me a numbing chest bump. "Is this fire or what?" he roared in my ear. "Nobody throws a party like The String!" He always talked about himself like he was talking about somebody else—somebody really great.

"Yeah, fire." Looking around, I had to admit it. The living room was packed with kids dancing, bouncing up and down to the beat, because there wasn't enough space to move side to side. Every hand held a soda can or water bottle, filling the air with a fine spray that came down like mist. Half-eaten pizza slices covered every surface in the house—tables, chairs, couches. I could feel, but not see, the layer of chip crumbs covering the carpet. The McBeans were going to have a major cleanup on their hands once this party ended—if it ever did. It showed no sign of slowing down. And now that the head of the P.A.G. was here, things could really go off the chain.

I followed a conga line into the kitchen, where the pizza boxes were stacked to the ceiling and kids were starting to help themselves to slices of a six-foot hero sandwich. The clock on the microwave provided a depressing reminder that I should have been eleven minutes into my stream. What if the five followers I didn't know got discouraged and stopped following me? Gamers weren't very patient. They were used to nonstop action.

My eyes fell on the kitchen door, which led to String's backyard. Escape—that was the plan. I could be home in five minutes and online in another two. This party was so jam-packed and crazy that no one was going to notice that I'd walked in, walked through, and walked out. All they'd remember was that they'd seen me.

I fist-bumped Kelly Hannity, slipped between two girls who were eating half-melted ice-cream cake with chopsticks, and stepped through the door.

Grass under my feet. Freedom.

A very large hand closed on my shoulder. "Hi, Cam." The deep voice moved air.

Xavier. What was he doing outside the party instead of inside it?

He thrust a shoebox into my arms. "This is for you."

"Shoes?"

In answer, he tipped open the lid so I could see into the box. It was piled high with sugar cookies, each one decorated with a little flower drawn in pink and white icing.

"Uh—thanks," I managed.

"I baked them myself," he informed me proudly. "My mom had to help crack the eggs."

Who knew that cracking eggs was so much harder than cracking skulls? "They're great. But I'm going to get pretty fat eating all these."

"They're not for *eating*," Xavier explained. "They're for the P.A.G."

I was mystified. "Why does the P.A.G. need cookies?"

"To *sell*," he insisted. "For the fund-raiser. Remember, Mr. Fanshaw said . . ."

That explained a lot. If Mr. Fan-whatever had said it, for sure I'd paid no attention at all. Whenever the P.A.G.'s faculty adviser opened his mouth, my brain went into hibernation mode. Although I did remember something called the New Approach. If you sent all 874 paggers out to do community service, so many middle schoolers had a fifty-fifty chance of wrecking the place they were supposed to serve.

So the P.A.G. was switching to fund-raising for good causes. Instead of helping people directly, we would give them money so they could help themselves. For example, the Sycamore Public Library needed a new building on account of the fact that the old one had been condemned by the town engineers. It was really just an old mansion, built in the 1800s. The fact that it hadn't collapsed decades ago was a miracle. In my opinion, the part that really should have been condemned was their video game collection, which was so old that if you wanted a system to play it on, you'd have to dig it out of a time capsule.

Xavier's cookies were to meant to be sold at a P.A.G. fund-raiser for the library. There was a chance that I was supposed to be planning the fund-raiser, since I was president of the P.A.G. That's why Xavier gave the cookies to me instead of someone who had the faintest idea what to do with them.

There was no way I could escape now—not with Xavier breathing down my neck. So I thanked him and headed back into the house to search for another exit.

Navigating the crowd while holding the shoebox in front of me was practically impossible. I barely managed to get the box down on a kitchen counter so it wouldn't get battered and crushed. One thing I never wanted to have to do was to tell Xavier that his hard work had never lived to earn money for the library.

Almost everyone I bumped into asked about the big fund-raiser I was working on. The more people I talked to, the more depressed I became. It just served to remind me how the P.A.G. was holding back my streaming career.

Pavel grabbed me by the arm. "Dude, where have you been?" he hissed. "Wait till you hear this—"

I cut him off. "Can't it wait? I've got to get home to my stream!"

"No!" he insisted. "Technically, this is world-changing."

"Will you cut it out with the 'technically'—"

Then I spotted it, and my entire chain of thought disappeared in a puff of smoke. The lid of the shoebox sat beside it on the kitchen counter. A small crowd had gathered around, a forest of arms reaching inside. Pink flowered cookies were disappearing into mouths at an alarming rate. Out of the corner of my eye, I spied Xavier stepping in from the backyard. If he saw this . . .

I turned my back on Pavel and lunged for the counter.

"Where are you going?" Pavel wailed.

There was no time to answer. Xavier was only one long stride away. And the cookie box? Empty.

All I could do was get the lid back on to hide the fact that the cookies were gone. At the last second, I tossed my phone in there just in case Xavier nudged the box and didn't feel his cookies rattling around. Yes, I knew—one phone didn't equal a load of baked goods. But there was no time to think it through. Anyway, it had to be better than nothing.

With Xavier a few people behind me in the kitchen, I had no choice but to push out into the mobbed living room. Now that I didn't have any more cookies to worry about, I used the shoebox as a battering ram. More high fives and hugs, but the good news was that String was nowhere in sight. A Plan B formed in my mind: I would plow straight through the heart of the party and out the front door.

I almost made it. By the time I hit the front foyer, I had the shoebox out in front of me like a cowcatcher. The front door yawned open directly in front of me. Only two people blocked my way.

"Cam—we've been looking all over for you!"

Chuck—my other best friend, the third member of the Awesome Threesome. With him was Daphne Leibowitz, who'd been the first person to join the P.A.G. without knowing it was a fake club. In my mind, I always blamed her for what had happened. But I also gave her credit, because the P.A.G. wasn't all bad; it was just all bad for my lifestyle.

"We've got big news," Daphne announced with a wink at Chuck.

It was never good when Daphne had big news. Chuck knew that as well as I did, but you couldn't tell from the goofy grin on his face.

"We're a ship," he said, beaming.

"What—like the *Titanic*?" I asked.

"A *relation*ship," Daphne corrected. "We're going out."

Chuck put an arm around her, looking as proud as I'd ever seen him.

It took me a split second to realize that the crash I heard was just in my head. It was the sound of the entire world turning upside down.

At that very instant, the cookies rang. I was so stunned by the Chuck and Daphne bombshell that I fumbled my phone out of the shoebox. As it fell, I read the caller ID—Pavel, probably trying to warn me about the big announcement and save me a nasty shock.

The phone hit the tile floor with a bang. I scrambled to pick it up. Distorted by a jagged screen crack, Pavel's caller ID disappeared and was replaced by the picture of my streaming setup. The gaming part was blank, but there was a new posting on the comment feed. I squinted to read it: *Why isn't anything happening? This stream stinks! UNFOLLOW!*

If there was a word no streamer ever wanted to see, it was that one.

I had to do something about the P.A.G. My lifestyle depended on it.

CHAPTER TWO
CHUCK KINSEY

Why couldn't Pavel and Cam be happy for me? If one of them had been the first of the Awesome Threesome to get a girlfriend, I would have been happy for him.

Just jealous, I guess. I could relate. Having a girlfriend was so amazing that I could totally see how not having one could make a guy crabby. I wouldn't have known that a week ago—before Daphne and I started going out. But I'd changed a lot in those seven days.

I wasn't mad at them. They couldn't help it. Besides, if it hadn't been for Cam and the P.A.G., I never would have gotten close to Daphne in the first place. I'd never forget that big snowstorm in February when she'd brought a bunch of paggers to shovel off the beaver habitat we'd built for Elvis. The P.A.G. had still been banned back then, so we couldn't get a bus to take us. We had to walk the whole way, and it was, like, twelve degrees. We cleared away the snow, but Daphne was afraid that Elvis might have frozen to death in his lodge. Beavers don't hibernate, but they're really low energy in the winter months.

She used her finger to make a peephole, but she couldn't see anything because her glasses were all fogged up from the cold. So she raised the frames to peer inside, and for the first time, I noticed that she had beautiful eyes.

"Oh, barf!" was Pavel's opinion when I explained how it had happened. "I've seen Daphne without her glasses, too. They're eyes, same as everybody else has."

The last part he mumbled past a mouthful of gummy worms. We were at Sweetness and Light, our usual after-school hangout.

"Come on, guys," I wheedled. "Don't be that way. You like Daphne."

Cam made a face like his gummy worms were turning into real worms halfway down his throat. "Okay, we like Daphne—from a distance. Never forget that she was the first one to tell Mr. Fan-whatchamacallit about the Positive Action Group."

I was blown away. "How could you, of all people, complain about that? Sure, it wasn't what you originally planned, but the P.A.G. turned into the greatest thing ever. You can't blame Duckne for that."

Pavel choked. "Duckne?"

I could feel my face reddening. "It's our ship name. Daphne came up with it. You know, Daphne and Chuck—Duckne."

"You poor slob," Pavel said sadly. "Your life is technically over."

"Does she at least let you play video games?" Cam asked.

"Of course I play video games!" I exploded. "Who knows that better than you? You're the guys I play them with. We're still the Awesome Threesome. Nothing's changed except that Daphne will be around a lot, so we'll be more like a foursome."

"Not going to happen," Pavel said with conviction.

"Sure it is." I checked my watch. "She should be here any minute."

"Here?" Pavel's eyes bulged. "You invited her here? To *our* place?"

"I had to," I reasoned. "It's our *weekaversary*. We've been going out for seven whole days."

Pavel was furious. "Do our traditions mean nothing to you? I've spent three-quarters of a million dollars on gummy worms in this place."

"What difference does it make?" Cam told him wearily. "If I can't get my streaming career going, who cares if Daphne comes to Sweetness and Light?"

"Fine," Pavel muttered. "She can come. But no gummy worms. She can have any other candy, but gummy worms are off-limits. Some things have to stay sacred."

I looked to Cam for confirmation and got nothing. He'd been in a weird mood all day. The streaming thing was really getting him down. He was the best gamer of the Awesome Threesome, so he probably figured that his stream would take off and be an instant success. But it was turning out to be a lot harder than that. With 873 paggers all looking to him to be their leader, there just weren't enough hours in the day. Building an online following took time.

I tried to make him feel better. "Having a girlfriend isn't all fantasticness, either. I mean, it's fantastic, but that's the problem. It's distracting. You know that science quiz we got back today?" I took the test paper from my jacket pocket and laid it on the table between our three cups of candy. My grade delivered the unhappy message: *11/50.*

Pavel, who never got a grade below A-plus-plus, snorted. "Didn't you study?"

I was shamefaced. "Daphne wanted to go ice-skating."

"You should lend your test paper to Cam," Pavel told me sarcastically. "With grades like that, he'd be ineligible to be P.A.G. president."

"Yeah," Cam agreed glumly. "Too bad I'm not as dumb as Chuck."

"Nobody is," Pavel insisted. "He's dating Daphne."

"Hey—!"

I was about to stick up for my girlfriend when suddenly Cam was on his feet, wild-eyed, babbling so excitedly that

I could barely understand him. He kept repeating, "That's it! That's it!"

"What's it?" Pavel demanded.

He was chortling with glee. "If I was flunking, I wouldn't be allowed to be the head of the P.A.G.!"

"Yeah, but you're *not* flunking," I pointed out.

"I don't have to fail for real," he reasoned. "I just have to *tell* everybody I'm failing. Then somebody else will be forced to run the P.A.G. And I'll have the time I need to get my stream up and running."

Pavel looked at him with respect. "That could work, you know. Technically."

"It's genius!" I approved. "You'll have the perfect excuse to disappear if you're bringing your grades up."

"Chuck and I will help," Pavel put in.

"And Daphne," I added.

You would have thought I'd threatened them with an ax.

"Don't even *think* about telling Daphne what I'm doing," Cam said in a voice like cold steel.

"Why not? She can help! She's smart!"

"She may be smart," Cam retorted, "but she's got a big mouth. Like if she got laryngitis, all the other bigmouths in the world would move up one space. If she spills the beans that I'm lying about bad grades so I'll have extra gaming time, my name will be mud."

I was offended on Daphne's behalf. "You're calling my girlfriend a rat! And for something she hasn't even done!"

"The thing is," Pavel explained, "Daphne's not a gamer like us, so she won't get why streaming is so important. She'll see this plan as us tricking everybody."

"And she has a big mouth," Cam added feelingly.

I definitely should have stuck up for Daphne a little better. On the other hand, what Pavel said made sense. Daphne was great and all that. But once she made a decision about something, though, you couldn't stop her with a bulldozer. It was a good quality—most of the time. Look at what she'd done for Elvis. He'd been the town pest, abandoned by the beaver colony, chewing on people's fences and siding. By the time she got through with him, he had a nicer habitat than the mayor. Her heart was always in the right place. Still, I couldn't risk her exposing Cam.

Then again . . . "Daphne says there should be no secrets in a relationship," I told them.

"This isn't a secret," Pavel reasoned. "It's a covenant that binds the Awesome Threesome."

I didn't know what *that* was, and I didn't want to know. "So long as I'm not keeping secrets," I said.

The bell over the door tinkled and there she was. My girlfriend. Those words still seemed strange and wonderful. She beamed at me and I couldn't help noticing that she really *did* have kind of a big mouth. You could probably fit a hockey puck in there. Then I remembered that the reason her smile was so wide was because she was seeing me. That made me feel warm all over.

"Hi, guys!" She rushed to our table, but before she could grab a gummy worm, Pavel slid my cup just out of her reach.

"A girl, you have!" announced Mrs. Backward, owner of Sweetness and Light. Her real name was Mrs. Bachman. We called her Backward because of the way she talked—with everything in reverse, kind of like Yoda. She approached our table, smiling at Daphne. "I should bring you what?"

"Oh, I'll just share with Chucky," Daphne replied airily.

Pavel shot me a look that would have qualified as a deadly weapon in most civilizations.

"You know, Mrs. B," I put in quickly, "I'm not feeling gummy worms today. Bring us an order of gummy bears."

Pavel nodded approvingly.

Mrs. B's eyebrow shot up. "Adventurous, you are. Your mind, you changed."

"Just felt like a little variety," I managed stiffly. The Awesome Threesome had been strictly worms-only at Sweetness and Light since we'd started coming in the third grade.

Daphne sat down, sharing half my chair. I loved it.

"So, what's new with you guys?" she asked.

Pavel spoke up, his expression tragic. "The news is not good. Tell her, Cam."

"No!" Cam shook his head stubbornly. "I'm not telling anyone. If people find out, they won't let me be president of the P.A.G."

Daphne's smile disappeared. "What are you talking about?"

I couldn't stand to watch those guys setting her up for the big lie. So I just blurted it out: "Cam's flunking eighth grade!"

"What?" Her horrified eyes fell on my science quiz on the table. Pavel had his thumb over my name. But you could see the grade at the top: *11/50.*

"Oh, Cam, I'm so sorry!"

"It's the P.A.G.," Pavel explained. "His duties as president monopolize so much of his day that there's no time left for anything else."

Daphne leaped up, which caused me to tumble off my half of the chair onto the hard floor. "Well, not anymore!" she stated decisively. "Cam, I'll take over the P.A.G. work until you get your academics in order. Where do we stand on the library fund-raiser?"

"We had a box of cookies," Cam confessed, "but they got eaten by mistake—"

"Don't say another word," Daphne interrupted. "I'll handle everything. It might cut into my time with Chucky, but I'm sure he won't mind."

As I hauled myself up off the floor, Pavel snuck me a wink.

I minded a lot.

CHAPTER THREE
CAMERON BOXER

It was a pretty ill plan. I arrived at school on Monday morning, totally amped to spread the word about how I was tanking in my classes.

The more I thought about the idea, the more I liked it. I wasn't a terrible student, but flunking was at least as good a match for me as leading the school. And if it gave me the breathing room to get the stream going, it was the right move all around.

As usual, Pavel had some advice. "Don't lay it on too thick about how dumb you are. Remember, the kids in this school think you're a genius for creating the P.A.G. Focus on the time angle—your grades are suffering because you're too busy."

Chuck had another concern. "I don't like how Daphne got mixed up in all this. It's bad enough that we're not telling her the truth. But now she's stuck organizing the whole library fund-raiser."

"Are you kidding?" Pavel crowed. "Daphne lives for this kind of stuff. She probably lines up sheep in her sleep. Telling other people what to do is her favorite thing in the world. Running a whole fund-raiser is her dream. Chances are, she'll even figure out a way to work Elvis into it. You know, *Support the library and upgrade the beaver habitat to a condominium.*"

"Daphne's been kind of worried about Elvis lately," Chuck admitted glumly. "He's too skinny. Beavers are supposed to fatten up once winter's over. At least, that's what it says on Wikipedia."

We entered the school. "If having a girlfriend means I have to memorize the Wikipedia page on beavers," I commented, "then I'm staying single forever."

I scanned the crowded hallway, wondering how long it would be before some pagger hit me up for fund-raiser details. That person, I decided, would be the next to hear the sob story about my failing grades.

In my mind, I counted down: 10 . . . 9 . . . 8 . . .

Felicia Hochuli ran up to us. But instead of asking about the P.A.G., she threw her arms around me. "We're with you all the way, Cam," she said emotionally, then hurried off.

I was stunned. "What was *that*?"

Chuck shrugged. "Maybe you're getting a girlfriend, too."

"No, that can't be it," Pavel commented. "She looked— sympathetic. Like your dog died or something."

A sixth-grade boy I didn't recognize was next. He grabbed my hand and shook it, like we were at a funeral. "That's really rough, Cam. Good luck."

From then on, it was a parade. By the time I got to my locker, at least a dozen people had come up to me to pledge their support. A few of them even apologized, as if they were the cause of my troubles.

"For what?" I said aloud as Tavon Woods disappeared into the crowd outside the library.

"Cam—I came as soon as I heard." String sprinted along the row of lockers, sweaty from his off-season football workout. "When I got kicked off the team for bad grades, the P.A.G. was there for me, and The String is going to be there for you. Anything you need—I've got your back."

"Bad grades?" I echoed. That's what this was about! Here I was about to start the rumor about my academic problems and it was already all over the building.

"When Daphne told me you were flunking out, it hit me like an illegal chop block," String went on. "It was like a blindside tackle—except that the tackler isn't born yet who can catch up with The String. When Xavier heard the news, he head-bumped his locker. Looks like somebody took a sledgehammer to it . . ."

My eyes met Pavel's and Chuck's. We didn't have to spread anything; Daphne had done our spreading for us.

"Well, Chucky, what did we tell you?" Pavel announced after String had moved on. "Your girlfriend really *does* have the biggest mouth in Sycamore."

"Quit saying that," Chuck growled.

"No, it's a good thing," I insisted. "Who knows how long it would have taken the three of us to get the word out. But telling Daphne is better than taking out a front-page ad in the *New York Times*."

Chuck couldn't help looking a little proud. For sure, he was 100 percent behind Daphne, who already had the library fund-raiser half planned by the late bell. Chuck followed her around like an adoring puppy. This was barely week two of the good ship Duckne, and he had already changed. He had a new haircut. He dressed differently; he tucked in his shirt. He wore so much Axe body spray that you could smell him coming five minutes before he walked into a room. He was almost like a mutant version of himself—but as long as he supported my streaming, I didn't care.

By the weekend, I was exactly where I belonged, controller in hand, setting up the greatest live game stream in Internet history.

There were a couple of complications. First, this was a *new* stream. I had to close my first account, because I couldn't use my real name anymore. I'd never get away with fobbing off my P.A.G. responsibilities when any idiot could find me on the Internet while I was supposed to be pulling up my grades. All those paggers were picturing me hitting the books, not playing video games online for the audience of thousands I intended to have.

If my name was a problem, my face was an even bigger one. No point in using an alias if I could be recognized. I had to stream in disguise. I tried on an old Mario getup I used to wear for Halloween, but it didn't really fit anymore. Besides, it was so hot in there that it might have affected my performance.

Pavel had a better idea. He took the black mask from my sister Melody's Zorro costume and tied it around my head. It was comfortable and light, and the eyeholes were big enough for a clear view of the screen.

"How do I look?" I asked.

"Your own mother wouldn't recognize you," he promised.

That left just my voice needing a disguise. "There's only one way for a member of the Awesome Threesome to take care of that," Pavel announced. He took a gummy worm from a ceramic bowl and shoved it into my mouth, burying it into my right cheek. Then he tucked another one into my left. Zorro looked like he had the mumps. Better still, he sounded nothing like me—garbled and a little slurpy.

"Keep the bowl close," Pavel advised. "You'll need new gummy worms when these start to dissolve. You're going to put away a lot of candy by the time you get to 50,000 subscribers."

"It's a sacrifice I'm willing to make," I told him with a grin.

He helped me get set up in front of the console and the webcam, checking to make sure the screen looked perfect for anyone following online.

It was zero hour. All I needed was a name.

"How about *The Fox*?" Pavel suggested.

"Why fox?" I asked.

"The mask," he explained. "Weren't you paying attention in Spanish class? *Zorro* means *fox*."

That was how I became GameFox229. It sounded just right for the name of a mega-popular streamer. The 229 part was a tribute to Draja Dubrovnik, the greatest gamer of all time. He was born on leap year day—February 29. If I could be even half as good as him, I'd get to 50,000 subscribers in record time.

When I clicked the button that took me live, it was like opening the door to a brave new world.

Because I was starting from scratch, no one was watching at first. My phone was still subscribed to the old stream, so I wasn't even following myself. Luckily, Pavel ran straight home and logged in on his computer, which brought the counter up to one. Chuck would have doubled that, but he was busy somewhere being half of Duckne.

I forced myself not to let that get me down. I was a gamer; this was a game, and playing it to the best of my ability was as natural as breathing. "It's World War Two, and I'm leading a band of Norwegian freedom fighters," I narrated around the gummy worms in my mouth. It sounded a little garbled, but hopefully people would think it was my Scandinavian accent. "Our mission is to blow up the Vemork heavy water plant. If we fail, the Nazis might develop the atomic bomb first and change the course of history . . ." Sugary goop dribbled down my chin. But with the controller in my hands, there wasn't much I could do about it.

We parachuted to the mountainside through a howling blizzard and skied through dense forest, our backpacks stuffed with high explosives. The factory was heavily guarded, but we didn't dare use our guns. Any loud noise would bring dozens of soldiers down upon us.

As I crept up behind a sentry, my knife in my teeth, I couldn't help noticing that my followers had already zoomed up to six. I even had my first comment on the message feed. It read: *This stream rocks!!!* Oh—my heart sank a little—that was from Pavel. But it still counted. And anyway, I'd have more comments than I knew what to do with when I blew the Vemork plant sky-high.

"I hope nobody minds the sight of a little blood, because look out," I told my followers, twirling the joystick. In the game, that operated my Mark II combat knife.

A loud pounding at the door shook the house. It broke

my concentration so suddenly that I lifted three inches off the couch and one of the gummy worms almost went down the wrong pipe. On the screen, a sentry smacked my knife away with the barrel of his machine gun and brought the butt down on my head. The Norwegian forest began to spin as my character went down in the snow. Choking and spitting, I barely managed to pause the game before being surrounded and captured by the enemy.

The pounding went on upstairs. *"Cam! It's me! Let me in!"* I recognized Chuck's voice.

"Go away!" I shouted.

In horror, I realized my mistake. What if my followers thought I wanted them to leave? "Not you guys!" I babbled, as the counter clicked down until there were only two people left. "I—I—we're experiencing technical difficulties. Please stand by!" And GameFox229 went offline.

Still choking a little, I raced upstairs with murder in my heart. I threw open the door and glared out at Chuck. "You *idiot*—"

My tantrum fizzled as my eyes fell on the pet carrier in his arms. Brown fur, beady eyes, big buckteeth. "Wait a minute. Is that—?"

"Elvis," Chuck finished, inviting himself inside, beaver and all. "I wanted you to see him. He really is too skinny, right?" He frowned. "What's up with the mask?"

I didn't hit him. I deserved a lot of credit for that. "I'm

starting the new stream today, remember? At least I was trying to before fifty percent of Duckne showed up with a stupid rodent!" I wheeled on him and raced back downstairs to my streaming setup. Zero followers. They were all gone, even Pavel.

"Sorry, Cam." Chuck followed behind me, shamefaced. "It's just that Daphne's really upset. I want to be a good boyfriend, but what do I know about beavers? Fat beavers, thin beavers—it's all the same to me. Yeah, I guess Elvis looks kind of skinny, but maybe I just think that because I want to support Daph. I need your unbiased opinion."

There was a rustling in the pet carrier. Elvis pressed his face up against the bars, staring at my screen, mesmerized by the colorful video game images. Yeah, sure, what did a beaver know? He had no idea he was looking at a frozen picture of my character being captured by guards outside a Nazi heavy water plant in 1942.

"I'm going back to my stream," I told Chuck, my voice under tight control. "There may still be somebody watching—although I doubt it after you made me mess up. As for the skinny beaver, ask yourself if the kind of person who cares about that is someone you want to be. Because the Chuck Kinsey I know isn't that kind of person. At least he wasn't until he got himself mixed up in a 'ship.'"

Chuck got quiet. "You're picking on Daphne and I don't appreciate it."

"I'm not picking on Daphne," I countered. "Daphne obsessing over Elvis is totally normal. What's not normal is when *you* do it."

"Fine. I'm leaving."

"Make sure you close the door on your way out," I called, settling myself back into streaming position, behind console and computer.

All the way up the stairs, Elvis's eyes never left the screen. And when the carrier was hefted out of view, he protested with a high-pitched whine that sounded like a crying baby. I heard the door slam.

I felt bad about kicking out a friend, but these moments when I had the entire house to myself were prime streaming time. Chuck understood that as well as anybody.

As it was, I had my work cut out for me. I had to escape from the guard, who had a machine gun, while I had nothing but the thousands of hours I'd put into this game. A little-known hack—I held down the R and L buttons and tapped the on/off switch. Suddenly, my character whirled around and delivered a paralyzing kick. The sentry went down, but before he could shoot, my team of freedom fighters burst through the bushes and took him out.

"The mission is back on!" I narrated to my audience of zero.

No, wait—three of them were back! I stuffed fresh gummy worms into my cheeks and went to work. As we entered the Vemork plant, battling guards and planting explosive charges, I watched the counter of followers tick slowly upward: 5 . . . 8 . . . 11. Double digits! Okay, it was no 50,000, but this was only day one, after all. And I'd gotten off to a bad start back there in the forest.

I had comments, too—enough to fill an entire pane of my streaming screen. People were loving it! A few even wanted to know how I'd pulled off my spectacular escape. "Tricks of the trade," I explained. "A magician never reveals his secrets." With my fresh mouthful of gummy worms, the word came out "shecretsh" along with a dollop of spit on the carpet. I made a mental note to tell Mom Melody did it. Melody didn't play video games anymore, so I'd have to be super convincing.

"Explosive charges placed and ready, sir," my lieutenant reported.

What a triumph! To come back from capture to this glorious moment could be the greatest achievement of my entire gaming career. And to have it happen in front of my very first streaming audience made my heart swell with pride.

I was about to give the order to blow the place to smithereens, when I became aware of a sound I'd never heard before. It wasn't loud exactly, but it was kind of grating, and close by, too—right outside the basement window. A rough noise, like people crushing crackers into their soup.

I took a few seconds to crane my neck and check it out. The delay could only add to the suspense of my followers who were waiting for the big kablooey.

At first, I saw nothing out the high window, but then I caught a glimpse of a broad, flat brown tail. There were two options: Either a duck-billed platypus had swum here from the east coast of Australia, or Elvis was back.

"Hang on a sec," I told my viewers, slipping off the couch. It didn't sound very Norwegian, but this was an emergency. I hoisted myself up to the windowsill and peered outside. It was the beaver, all right. He might not have been fat enough to suit Daphne Leibowitz, but he was making up for it by chewing on the cedar shakes that covered our wall.

The dilemma nearly tore me in two. On one hand was the Vemork heavy water plant, which had to go. The entire direction of the war depended on it. On the other, how could I sit by while a wild animal ate our house?

I paused the game again. It was going to cost me followers, but I couldn't let Mom and Dad come home to find the back wall missing up to beaver height.

I ran outside and circled around the house to confront that little terrorist. "Scram! Bad beaver! Go home! Shoo!"

He must have thought I said *chew*, because he kept right on doing it, even when I stomped my foot on the ground right next to him. He was either fearless or stupid. Or it was possible that our house was really, really delicious.

I did the only thing I could think of: I picked him up. I guess I was hoping he'd run away when I reached for him. But Elvis was so used to having the P.A.G. around fussing over him that he wasn't afraid of people anymore.

So what now? I felt like the dog who chases a car and has absolutely no idea what do when he catches it. I could only think of one thing: My audience was waiting. My game console was waiting. World War II was waiting. When I burst back into the house and down to the basement, the fact that I was still holding a beaver barely registered with me. I dumped Elvis on the floor, reinserted myself into the streaming spot, and unpaused the game.

"Showtime, folks!" I announced, and hit the button to detonate the charges.

The Vemork heavy water plant went up like the Fourth of July. It was everything I'd hoped for and more—a magnificent supernova of victory for the good guys. Only—the billowing smoke and flame cleared to reveal the counter. Zero. All my followers had deserted me again. The greatest, most amazing explosion in the annals of online gaming, and nobody was there to see it but me—and Elvis. The beaver had climbed up onto the couch and was watching with rapt interest.

"Go away," I told him. "You ruined everything."

He didn't budge.

Fine, let him stay. At least when he was sitting here with me, he wasn't devouring our house. I'd figure out what to do with him later—probably when Mom and Dad got home and found a giant rodent in their basement.

I started a new mission, determined to earn back some of my lost followers. Nobody was going to come between me and my lifestyle—especially not a dumb beaver.

CHAPTER FOUR
PAVEL DYSAN

I couldn't believe what I was seeing. What was happening on the computer screen in front of me was (technically) impossible, but how could I ignore the evidence of my own eyes? Even when the doorbell rang, I backed up all the way to answer it so I wouldn't miss anything.

Chuck stood on the doorstep, sweaty and disheveled, lugging an empty pet carrier. "What took you so long, man? I'm dead! I'm totally dead!"

"Calm down," I soothed. "What's the matter?"

"I lost Elvis!" he mourned. "Daphne's going to kill me!"

"Come with me," I told him.

"No, man!" He was practically hysterical. "I took Elvis over to Cam's to get a second opinion on how skinny he is. But I didn't close the cage right, and on the way back, he busted out and took off on me. I've been searching for the past hour. He's capital-G Gone. Now Daphne just texted. She wants to meet at the habitat. What am I going to do?"

"Come," I repeated, this time dragging him by the arm.

He stopped dead the minute he caught sight of the computer. It was logged on to the GameFox229 stream. On the screen, a battle scene raged on the rough terrain of a snow-covered mountainside. In the window to the left was the gamer himself—Cam in his Zorro mask, his fingers just a blur on the controller.

That wasn't the incredible part.

What was really amazing was the second figure perched on the back of the sofa, staring over Cam's shoulder in intense concentration. Nose wiggling, brown fur, buckteeth—

"Elvis!" Chuck practically howled. "What's he doing at Cam's?"

"He must have run back there when he escaped from the carrier," I suggested.

"But *why*?"

"I'm no animal expert, but I think he likes video games. Look at his eyes. He's following the action." A rapid *whump-whump-whump* sounded over the audio. "And I think he slaps his tail when he gets excited."

"Well, he can't stay!" Chuck exclaimed. "Daphne's meeting me at the habitat in fifteen minutes, and if there's no Elvis, she's going to freak."

"Hey, check it out. The message feed is going crazy." I leaned closer to the screen. Comments scrolled down the right side like a waterfall:

That doesn't look like a GameFox or any other kind of fox . . .

What is it, a woodchuck?

It's a beaver, stupid. Look at those teeth.

Don't you recognize a capybara when you see one?

Beaver. Definitely beaver.

So why GameFOX?

It went on and on.

"Come on, Pavel," Chuck wheedled. "You've got to help me."

"Fine," I agreed. "But you have to admit it isn't every streamer who's got a beaver hanging over his shoulder like he's coaching."

"Pa-vel!" He was already at the door.

I couldn't resist rubbing it in. "You must be really scared of Daphne. You know, technically, healthy relationships shouldn't be based on fear. On the other hand, your girlfriend *is* kind of scary—"

"You wouldn't let me tell Daphne what's going on with Cam's streaming life," he shot back defiantly. "Well, this is part of that. If she gets the whole P.A.G. searching for Elvis . . ."

He had me there. Cam was keeping a secret, and the last thing he needed was Daphne nosing around.

We got on our bikes and pedaled to the Boxer home.

Melody answered the door. "Oh, hi. He's playing video games, big surprise." Her eyes found the pet carrier in Chuck's arms. "What's that for?"

"This?" Chuck held it up. "How did this get here?"

Melody was instantly alert. She stormed down the stairs. "Cam, why are Frick and Frack up there with—"

An earsplitting scream tore through the house. Chuck dropped the carrier in shock. It hit the floor and the door popped open. A split second later, a streak of brown flashed up the stairs and into the cage. If I didn't know better, I'd almost swear that Elvis was trying to close the door behind himself.

I reached down and latched it. "Go!" I hissed.

Chuck didn't have to be told twice. Daphne was probably already on her way to the habitat.

We got back on our bikes and rode for the woods on the edge of town where the P.A.G. had built the beaver lodge. Chuck had the extra responsibility of balancing the carrier on his lap, bashing it with his knees as he pedaled. He looked terrified—but not half as terrified as Elvis had to be after that shriek had rousted him from his perch on the couch.

As we dropped our bikes by the path that led into the woods, a terrible sight greeted us: another bike. A pink one.

"Daphne," Chuck croaked.

"This is where the whole 'ship' thing gets you," I lectured. "I don't have a girlfriend, and as you can see, I'm totally cool, calm, and collected. But look at you. You're a wreck."

"What do we do?" Chuck pleaded.

I let him suffer for a couple of minutes. "All right," I said finally. "I'll go in and distract her and you sneak Elvis in the back way."

He was pathetically grateful.

With Chuck and the beaver keeping well behind and out of sight, I started into the woods. "Daphne!" I called. "Daphne, is that your bike?"

And there she was, stopped in the trail ahead of me, barely fifty feet from the creek where the P.A.G. had established Elvis's habitat. Another thirty seconds and Chuck would have been up that creek without a paddle.

I looked at her critically—the girl who had turned Chuck into a boyfriend. Call me crazy, but I actually saw it for a split second. She was petite, with a nice smile and big green eyes—or maybe they were just magnified behind her glasses.

"Oh, hi, Pavel," she greeted me. "Is Chuck with you?"

"No, he went ahead," I told her. "He was really anxious to get here."

Out of the corner of my eye, I spotted movement in the bushes off to my left as Chuck outflanked us en route to the habitat. I heard a thud and a muffled "oof!" (Good old Chucky never graduated ninja school.)

"What was that?" Daphne asked.

"Woodpeckers," I supplied, thinking on my feet.

I made sure to slow our pace to just above a crawl, so by the time we reached the habitat, there was Chuck, standing on the bank, watching Elvis paddling around happily.

Duckne had a reunion, which was pretty gross. I felt like I was intruding on a private moment.

"He's still skinny," Daphne said tragically. "And—wait a minute! What happened to his eyes?"

Chuck was nervous. "His eyes?"

"They're glazed over. You know, like a kid who's been watching too much TV."

Remind me to never try to sneak anything past Daphne Leibowitz.

CHAPTER FIVE
CAMERON BOXER

Mr. Fan-whosis ambushed me at my locker on Tuesday.

"Good morning, Cameron. I'd like a word with you in my office."

This was never a good thing. He was the faculty adviser for the Positive Action Group, and he had never quite figured out that it wasn't supposed to be a real club. That probably had a lot to do with the 873 people besides me who'd joined. Whatever the reason, he loved the P.A.G., and he loved me for being its founder.

"Well, Mr. Fan—uh, sir, I really should be getting to class—"

"You can spare me a few minutes," he said firmly.

What could I do? I followed him to his office, which was a tribute to the achievements of the P.A.G. The whole room was wallpapered with P.A.G. posters and photographs and news clippings of our amazing good deeds.

He sat down behind his desk. "We've had some excellent meetings lately. Too bad you haven't been able to make it to any of them."

"I've been really busy," I began vaguely.

"I get that. You're a busy kid—president of the P.A.G. But that should just mean that you're busy with the club."

I had no answer for him. The other kids at school probably assumed I was a no-show at those meetings because I was home studying in order to pull up my grades. But I couldn't say that to Mr. Fan-doohickey. He was faculty, so if he wanted to see my grades, all he had to do was call them up on his computer. And there they'd be, not flunking at all. That was the whole problem of talking with the guidance counselor. He wasn't a bad guy. I had nothing against him. But he always expected me to *do* things. And doing things that weren't gaming related didn't fit into my lifestyle.

"I think part of the reason is the library fund-raiser," I explained carefully. "Daphne has kind of taken that over. And, man, isn't she knocking it out of the park?"

"I wanted to speak to you about that, too," he continued. "I've been looking over the sign-up sheets for the different stations, and your name isn't on any of them. It's like you're not even planning to be there."

"Of course I'll be there. I'm the P.A.G. . . ." My face twisted. I didn't like the word *president*. It sounded like someone who did things. ". . . guy."

He smiled thinly. "I'm glad to hear that you're still our 'guy,' and that I'll be seeing you Saturday."

"Saturday?" I was stunned. "*This* Saturday?"

That upset him for some reason. "Don't you even know the date of your own fund-raiser?"

Well, of course I did. I knew it was *some* Saturday. I just wasn't too clear on which one. I should have figured Xavier wouldn't have baked those cookies six months in advance.

For the first time all day, I caught a break. The bell rang. I got out of there before he had a chance to say another word.

Saturday! Saturday was my best streaming day. Mom and Dad were at the store from morning till night, so all I had to deal with was Melody. And since she had given up video games, she hardly ever came down to the basement. After seeing Elvis that time, she might never come to the basement again.

But now I would have to waste some of my precious Saturday sitting outside a building you can't sit *inside* because the ceiling could come down on your head any minute. And all to keep Mr. Fan-thingamajig off my case.

The time away from streaming was going to hurt. That first day of GameFox229 had really shown me how big this could turn out to be. Oh, sure, it was up and down there for a while, especially with all the interruptions. But when I got going, I had over 200 followers at one point—and that was after losing my entire audience twice. I had so many comments that I couldn't read them and keep my eyes on the game.

Since then, though, everything had been blah. I usually didn't have more than a couple dozen followers at any time, and most of their messages weren't very positive. And even the audience I had seemed impatient, like if something great didn't happen pretty soon, they were going to bolt and watch some other streamer or maybe even a YouTube video of a cat drinking out of the toilet. It was discouraging. I just couldn't figure out what had changed.

Pavel shared his opinion. "I'll tell you what changed. That first day you had Elvis with you. You read the comments. Everybody was talking about him."

"Everybody was laughing at him," I amended. "And at me. 'You should change your name to GameBeaver229.' Very funny. 'Stick to gaming, kid. You're way too dumb to run a zoo.' What's that supposed to mean?"

Pavel shrugged. "What do you care why they were watching? All that matters is they *were*. And they were probably telling their friends—that's where the bigger numbers came from."

I made a face. "My lifestyle is gaming, not animals. Just because I streamed with Elvis once doesn't mean I liked it. He smells funny, his fur keeps itching my cheek through the Zorro mask, and when he poops, it rolls under the couch. Melody had to help me move the whole sofa to clean it up. She had a few things to say about that, let me tell you. I'm going to be loading the dishwasher and taking out the garbage for a long time to keep her from telling my folks."

Pavel folded his arms in front of him. "You're the one who said—and I quote—'I'd do *anything* to get to fifty thousand subscribers.' There are a lot of streamers out there, but you're the only one with a beaver."

I stared at Pavel. He was a smart guy—a straight-A student; someone you listened to. The Positive Action Group had been my idea, but it never could have happened without Pavel. He had been the one with the brains to hack into the school's website and plant the phony P.A.G. page in the middle of all the real teams and clubs.

Could he be right about this, too? Fifty thousand subscribers would be nothing less than a guarantee that my lifestyle could go on forever.

"We've got to get that beaver back as soon as possible," I said firmly.

It wasn't a decision I made easily. It would be a huge hassle taking Elvis back and forth from the habitat. Plus, we'd have to keep it a secret from all those paggers, who couldn't find out about my streaming—*and* from Mom and Dad.

The minute we presented the new plan to Chuck, he flipped out.

"Are you nuts?" he gasped. "Bring Elvis to your house *on purpose*? There's no way Daphne would ever go for that!"

"Since when does everything have to be approved by Daphne?" Pavel challenged. "Maybe that's how it works in boyfriend zone, but in the real world, you'd be amazed to find out that Daphne isn't in charge."

"Yeah, but it's, like, animal cruelty," Chuck protested.

"That's not what I saw on my computer," Pavel retorted. "I saw a rodent who was totally enthralled by what was on the screen in front of him. And if that's true, then the real cruelty would be *not* letting him watch."

"I guess so," Chuck conceded in a small voice. A barrage of Pavel's logic always made him dizzy.

"You've still got the pet carrier, right?" I added.

The trial run took place Thursday afternoon. Mom and Dad ran Boxer's Furniture Showroom, which was open late, so coast clear, parent-wise. Pavel, Chuck, and I made sure to ride our bikes to school, and Chuck brought the carrier, which we hid in the bushes. Then, at three thirty, we pedaled straight to the woods and hiked in to pick up Elvis.

The beaver was lounging on the banks of his pond, chewing on a twig, chowing down with gusto, the way he had when he'd been trying to eat my house.

"Still skinny," Chuck observed unhappily.

"You can't tell by his appetite," Pavel put in. "Maybe wood isn't very fattening. Daphne should get him to switch to cheesecake."

"Not healthy," Chuck clucked disapprovingly.

None of this was helping my streaming career. "All right, Elvis, saddle up," I announced.

Chuck placed the kennel on the ground in front of the beaver and opened the door invitingly.

I thought he'd scoot inside. Instead, he backed away.

I blamed Pavel. "You said he likes video games."

Pavel shook his head in disgust. "How's he supposed to know we're taking him to video games?"

Chuck picked up the half-eaten twig and tossed it into the cage. "There you go. There's your snack. Go get it."

Zero movement.

"Brilliant," Pavel said sarcastically. "I suppose you haven't noticed we're in a whole forest full of sticks technically just like that one."

"Have you got a better idea?" Chuck challenged.

I thought about what had gotten Elvis into the cage last time. I sucked in a lungful of air and let loose the loudest, most high-pitched screech I could manage. It wasn't as good as Melody's, but it did the trick. Elvis scrambled into the carrier so fast that he almost blasted out the opposite side.

Another step closer to 50,000 subscribers.

CHAPTER SIX
MELODY BOXER

I wasn't afraid to say it: I was a better gamer than my brother.

As my secret online identity—Evil McKillPeople—I stalked him all over the network, beating him at everything from *Age of Wonders* to *Zoo Tycoon*.

He knew it, too. And when he needed a partner for Rule the World, the big gaming tournament, he picked me.

I had the edge over Cam in every way except one: He *cared* a lot more than I did.

That was obvious. Cam cared more about gaming than anybody alive, and probably a lot of dead people, too. If our house got vaporized by an asteroid strike, he wouldn't even notice so long as the gaming console survived. The whole reason the P.A.G. got started was because Cam cared about video games so much—he needed Mom and Dad to believe he was getting a life, the kind that didn't operate by joystick.

It was Rule the World that put me over the top. To be trapped inside a convention center for three days with 10,000 clones of my brother—some of them in their forties! Don't get me wrong—it was fun. But when I got home after that weekend, my gaming interest was gone. I hadn't touched a controller since.

Good luck explaining that to Cam. To him, giving up gaming was like giving up breathing. My brother and I had never been best buddies. Now he looked at me as if I had just arrived from another planet.

"How could you give up video games?" he challenged. "You're *ill*!"

Believe it or not, I was kind of flattered. To Cam, being "ill" was the highest possible praise.

It still didn't make me want to pick up a joystick. "It's just not my thing anymore."

He didn't get it, and I was sick of trying to explain it. Communication between the two of us had dwindled to nothing—if you didn't count "Help me clean the beaver poop out from under the couch."

Sigh.

The thing was, our parents worked long hours, so we were thrown together a lot. Every day after school, we were both home on our own until the furniture store closed at nine. All the not talking was driving me crazy.

It suited Cam just fine, though. Silence helped him concentrate on you-know-what. I'd polish off my homework upstairs while he took over the couch potato spot in the dungeon. Now that he was streaming instead of just gaming, I had to try to tune out his overexcited commentary for his followers. I could only imagine the kind of person who had nothing better to do than to follow my brother. For sure, they had even less of a life than he did.

Cam usually got home before me. At three thirty, Sycamore Middle School's most dedicated student leader was usually poised like a sprinter by the nearest exit, ready to make a beeline for home and the game console. So on Thursday, I was surprised to let myself into an empty house.

I sat down at the kitchen table and started studying for the next day's science test. Maybe the Awful Threesome had gone to Sweetness and Light to gorge on gummy worms.

Suddenly, the door was practically kicked open. There was Cam, flanked by his two buddies. That pet cage was in his hand. And inside the cage—

"Oh, no you don't!" I exclaimed. "That smelly beaver isn't coming in here again."

"Come on, Mel," Cam pleaded. "You're a pagger, too. Elvis is almost like our mascot."

I wasn't buying it. "You can't snow me like you snow everybody else, Cam Boxer. I know for a fact that the pagger who has the *least* to do with the P.A.G. is you."

"I need him," Cam wheedled. "For my stream."

"Elvis has his own stream," I countered, misunderstanding on purpose. "Take him back to the woods so he can swim in it."

My brother scowled at me. "You know what I mean. My *gaming* stream. Elvis attracts attention."

"He attracts attention in the basement, too," I reminded him. "The attention of anybody with a nose. You wouldn't be trying this if Mom was here. Maybe we should give her a call . . ."

Pavel jumped in where he didn't belong. "We'll pay you."

That couldn't have been part of the plan, because Cam stared at him.

"Using what for money?" I scoffed.

"When Cam's gaming stream goes big time, he'll be rolling in cash," Chuck blustered.

This was getting interesting. "Twenty percent of everything you make on the stream," I demanded.

"That's highway robbery!" Pavel protested. "Twenty percent just to hide it from your parents? Cam, don't give her a penny more than ten."

"Ten not to tell Mom and Dad," I explained. "The other ten is to keep me from spreading it around school. I've been hearing a lot of rumors lately about how you're stepping back from the P.A.G. so you can be a serious student. Funny how the kids don't know anything about GameFox229."

Cam glared at me with burning eyes. "Fine," he rasped. "Twenty percent."

I wasn't an idiot. I totally understood that twenty percent of nothing was still nothing. There was no way anybody would pay real money to watch my brother play video games. I'd been watching him for free my whole life, and even at that price it wasn't worth it. A beaver wouldn't help. Maybe a T. rex.

"It's a deal," I told him.

The Awful Threesome Plus Beaver went to the basement and I returned to my science book. Pretty soon, though, it was impossible to concentrate. I was used to the video game noises, but Cam's overhyped commentary was really distracting:

"Retreat! That guy has a legendary bolt-action sniper! . . . Somebody drop me some wood! How can I build a fort with only seventy-five total materials! . . . How does my epic blue-pump shotgun do only eight damage? My electric toothbrush is a better weapon! . . ."

Even worse was this *whack-whack-whack* sound like those idiots were beating each other with Ping-Pong paddles.

I couldn't help myself. I had to go down there and have a look.

It was the strangest thing I'd ever seen. My masked brother was on the couch, controller in hand, gaming and shouting into a headset. Elvis perched on the back of the sofa, his squat body arched over Cam's shoulder, watching with intense concentration. So help me, he looked like he was really into it. When the gameplay was tense, he froze; when things got exciting, he slapped his tail against the fabric of the couch. That explained the *whack-whack-whack*.

But those dummies were right. Elvis drew a crowd. The counter showed over 100 followers, and the comment feed was lit up like a Christmas tree. I squinted at the laptop screen. None of it had anything to do with Cam's gaming or even the Zorro mask. It was all Elvis. Why was he there? What was his name? Was the beaver real, or was he some kind of Muppet? Why wasn't he a fox? Did he understand what he was watching or was he just faking it? Did Cam have to hire a special handler to teach him to appreciate video games?

Pavel and Chuck were whispering the questions so Cam could answer them as he streamed. It was a freak show. One commenter even wanted to know if Elvis was a trained cat inside a beaver suit.

I went back upstairs, but by then, my concentration was totally shot. Soon I was surfing the Internet, trying to find out if beavers were naturally drawn to TV images. There was nothing on the subject—and why would there be? How many beavers had access to video games? It took my brother and his half-witted friends to do the groundbreaking research.

Sigh.

I kept tiptoeing downstairs to check on them. After an hour, they switched games. Elvis seemed to enjoy extreme wrestling just as much as a battle royale. He even let out a series of squeaks when the wrestlers started beating each other up with steel chairs. By the time GameFox229 signed off, Cam had nearly 400 followers, and the messages were mostly exclamation points.

I caught sight of my reflection in the hall mirror. I couldn't begin to describe the expression on my face—part amazement, part disgust, and part diabolical grin.

Maybe my 20 percent of nothing wasn't so nothing after all.

CHAPTER SEVEN
CAMERON BOXER

With GameFox229 picking up new followers every time I streamed with Elvis, I was especially excited about Saturday. Weekend audiences were usually a lot bigger, and I was hoping to break my record—maybe even shatter it.

Unfortunately, Saturday was *the* Saturday—fund-raiser day. Pavel, Chuck, and Melody were all signed up to volunteer at the big event, which meant that I'd be gaming on my own. Worse, I'd promised Mr. Fan-doojig that I'd be there. How annoying was that? The most important day in my short streaming career, and I was going to have to waste precious time at some fund-raiser. It was another example of how the P.A.G. always managed to interfere with my lifestyle.

One bright spot: I'd told the guidance counselor that I'd go, but I never said for how long. Thirty seconds ought to do it—I was going to streak across the library lawn like a shooting star three minutes before the four p.m. closing.

I could still get in a full day of streaming. GameFox229 was priority number one.

Boxer's Furniture Showroom opened at eleven a.m. on Saturdays. Mom and Dad left for the store at ten thirty. Melody helped me put down the newspapers behind the couch, even though she didn't have to.

"I know you, Cam Boxer," she accused. "You'll forget, and Elvis will stink up the whole basement."

I would have been more offended, except that she was right. I'd forgotten already. I would have left to pick up Elvis without preparing the basement. And even if I remembered later, for sure I wouldn't have delayed my streaming for the sake of a little beaver poop. I had a kind of tunnel vision, so non-gaming details never registered with me. Melody considered this a negative, but it gave me the kind of focus I needed to turn GameFox229 into a success.

When I got to the beaver habitat, Elvis was sitting on the grassy bank like he was waiting for a bus. He seemed a little thrown by the fact that it was just me picking him up, but I was prepared for that. I pulled the Zorro mask out of my pocket and tied it over my face. The instant he saw that, he practically broke his neck hustling into the carrier.

I wasn't a huge fan of biking home with the cage balanced on my handlebars, and I was a little worried about attracting attention. But as it turned out, I didn't pass a single soul. The P.A.G. had gotten so big that the whole town basically shut down so everybody could go to the library fund-raiser.

I hit a minor snag when I turned onto our street and saw Dad's car in our driveway. The last thing I needed was to have to explain why I was bringing the beaver home. I barely managed to get out of sight behind our next-door neighbor's garage. I waited in agony, wondering if my breakout day of streaming was going to fall victim to something like a headache or an upset stomach. Elvis was antsy, too, and kept chewing on the bars of the kennel with those giant front teeth of his.

At last, Dad left with the brown bag lunches that must have been forgotten when my folks left for work this morning. The coast was clear.

By the time GameFox229 went live, there were already 150 people waiting online for me. My heart was pounding like a beat drop. I could feel their support egging me on as I launched into my first game, which was soccer. Elvis seemed to be a soccer fan. Or maybe he just liked it when I stretched *"Go-o-o-o-o-o-al!"* into a seven-syllable word— which wasn't easy with a mouth full of gummy worms. At one point, he actually climbed onto my shoulder and began whacking me in the back with his tail. It was amazing how much it hurt. I decided to switch to a street-racing game—at least until I could feel my spine again.

As the hours unfolded, my followers grew, until there were nearly 600. I could almost taste that this was the start of something huge. Time seemed to stand still—at least until I glanced at the clock. Yikes—it was 3:51. I'd promised Mr. Fan-diddly that I'd show up at the fund-raiser, and there were only nine minutes till closing!

I froze up—never a smart thing to do in the middle of a game. The Lamborghini I was driving slammed into a wall, and the explosion took out half a city block. It even scared Elvis, who had a high tolerance for game violence.

I was staring into the webcam like a deer in headlights. "I-I"—I stammered—"gotta go!"

I stuffed Elvis back in the carrier and ran out of the house like the police were after me. I leaped onto my bike and pedaled furiously for the woods. The digital time readout atop the Sycamore Bank building told the whole story: 3:55. There was no way I could drop Elvis off and make it to the fund-raiser in time. As it was, it would take a miracle for me to get to the old library before the P.A.G. shut everything down at four.

I blazed across town, moving at least as fast as the Lamborghini I'd just wrecked. Elvis squealed in agitation, slapping his tail against the side of the carrier.

"Cut it out, man!" I barked at him. "You'll put us in the ditch!"

I almost went into the ditch anyway when the library came into view. The place resembled the parking lot of the Super Bowl. Cars as far as the eye could see. Huge crowds swarming around food booths and sales tables. It was one minute to closing time!

I stashed Elvis's carrier in the bushes outside the post office next door. The beaver flashed me a resentful glare, which, believe or not, I could kind of relate to. To be snatched away from video games only to be stuffed into a leafy prison wasn't something I ever wanted to happen to me. Then I ran for the fund-raiser, trying to look like I'd been there for several hours.

The first face I saw was Pavel's. His jaw dropped in alarm and he gestured madly toward his cheek. In all the rush to get over here, I'd forgotten to take off the Zorro mask. I ripped it over my head and jammed it into my pocket.

"Why's everybody still here?" I demanded. "It's supposed to be ending now."

"Hey, Cam!" Chuck ran up to us. "Isn't this amazing? We're raking in a fortune, so Daphne gave the order to stay open an extra hour. She makes an amazing P.A.G. president, don't you think?"

"How'd GameFox go?" Pavel asked. "Any problems getting Elvis back in his habitat?"

"About that—" I began.

"Cam!" String exclaimed in his foghorn voice. He was wearing a greasy apron and working at a barbecue grill. He deftly flipped a burger onto a bun and held it out to me. "Have some sustenance, man. You must be starving from all that studying."

I was honestly so flustered that I forgot myself. "Studying?"

Pavel covered for me. "Our boy's been hitting the books all afternoon. Lousy way to spend a weekend."

"Eat," String commanded. "Nobody cooks burgers like The String." He dismissed the other food tables with a disdainful wave of his spatula. "Forget the rest, 'cause I'm the best."

So I ate it. What choice did I have? It was actually pretty good. As I chewed, String put an arm around me. "Listen, Cam, I can't tell you how much it means to the P.A.G. that you took time away from your schoolwork to support us. Oh, by the way, that'll be four bucks."

I didn't have a penny on me, so Chuck paid my tab. He was only too happy to boost the income for his girlfriend's fund-raiser.

From then on, it was a parade. Half the eighth grade, and a good chunk of the sixth and seventh, pulled me aside to thank me. And it wasn't the usual P.A.G. president stuff, either. Everybody went on and on about how impressed they were that I had put my urgent studying on hold to come to the library and support the team. Every single kid knew in his or her heart that there could not be a better leader than yours truly.

"Are you making progress?" Felicia asked earnestly. "Do you feel more in control heading into the midterm progress reports?"

I managed to nod. "But I've still got a long way to go," I added quickly. I didn't want people to think I'd be back at the helm of the P.A.G. anytime soon. GameFox229 was going great, but it would take a long time to get anywhere near 50,000 subscribers.

"Maybe I could help," she offered. "I'm great at English. I tutor elementary school kids in my neighborhood. And Jordan gets straight A's in science—"

"Absolutely not."

"But you've done so much for *us*." She was pleading now. "Let us return the favor."

"I have to do this on my own," I said firmly.

I couldn't miss the note of pride in Xavier's deep voice as he told me to take all the time off I needed. "Don't worry about the P.A.G.," he assured me, gesturing around the bustling property. "The fund-raiser's a smash hit." His heavy brow furrowed. "I didn't see my cookies over at the bake sale, though."

"They must have sold out first," I put in quickly. "Nobody can resist pink icing."

I made my way around the tables, being thanked and overappreciated. Mostly, I wanted to cross paths with Mr. Fan-yada-yada so I'd get credit for showing up. If I didn't, he might want to have another talk in his office.

Instead of the guidance counselor, I ran into the other 50 percent of Duckne.

Daphne's eyes narrowed at me. "What are you doing here?"

I told her what everybody had been telling me. "I'm taking time away from studying to support my fellow paggers."

"Not like that, you're not," she said sharply.

"Huh?"

"You're not helping the fund-raiser by walking around, doing nothing. Don't just stand there. Find a table and *work*."

"What table?" I challenged.

"*Any* one." She pointed to a long desk piled high with books and magazines. "How about the library overstock sale? Natalie's been working there all day. Give her a break."

I didn't enjoy being pushed around. Then I thought of Chuck, who got pushed around by Daphne full-time rather than just at the occasional fund-raiser, poor slob.

I wandered over to the desk and told Natalie to take the rest of the afternoon off. It wasn't as if we had any customers for old dog-eared books anyway. The fund-raiser was a mob scene, but the library overstock table was doing a nice quiet business of zero. It wasn't hard to see why. Our stock was pretty lame—outdated magazines, crossword puzzle books that were half filled in, scratched CDs of oompah music, and—

What was this? From the midst of the pile of old junk nobody wanted, a familiar illustration caught my eye. That was no CD case—it was a video game! And not just any game, but *Guardians of Geldorf*, one of my all-time favorites. I thought the only video games the library had were things like *Pong* and *Ms. PacMan, Grandpa Edition*. But *Guardians of Geldorf* was awesome—not new, but definitely a timeless classic. I must have spent a thousand joyous hours blasting Geldorfians out of their escape pods—that is, before our copy got thrown out, thanks to my stupid sister. When Melody gave up gaming, she tossed all her stuff, and *Guardians* must have been in there somewhere. Tragic.

And here was a new copy. Well, not new—ancient. It was only one dollar, which proved how dumb the library was, charging so little for a fantastic game.

Being flat broke, I whistled Pavel over and made him buy it for me.

"It's pretty beat-up," he observed critically. "Think it'll play?"

"It's a good omen," I decided. "For GameFox."

From the center table, by the library's front entrance, a woman's scream rang out. Suddenly, people were running, scattering in all directions. Someone jostled one of the food tables, and a large pyramid of Rice Krispies Treats toppled to the grass.

"What's going on over there?" Pavel wondered.

Warning shouts reached our ears, and more screams. The agitated customers began bumping into each other, and one side of the burger table collapsed, sending mustard, relish, and fixings sliding down the slope. I spotted String wheeling his barbecue grill out of harm's way for all the world like he was going out for a long pass. Xavier rescued a three-tiered cake—one of the raffle prizes—a split second before the pedestal was kicked out from under it. More tables began to go down, almost like a domino effect.

I turned to Pavel. "If you run into Mr. Fan-thingy, I was home studying the whole time." It wasn't worth getting credit for showing up if I might get blamed for something that wasn't even my fault.

Pavel wasn't paying attention. Instead, he was watching the chaos with analytical concentration. "It looks like everybody's running away from some kind of disturbance on the ground."

"What disturbance?" I asked.

Before the words were out of my mouth, Daphne

answered the question with a howl that echoed from one end of town to the other.

"El-vis!!"

Instinctively, I looked over at the flagpole next door. Sure enough, the overturned pet carrier stuck halfway out of the bushes, the door hanging open.

Okay, scratch the part about it not being my fault. At least I could share the blame with whoever had put such a weak door latch on the pet carrier, and with Mother Nature, who'd given beavers such powerful front teeth.

CHAPTER EIGHT
DAPHNE LEIBOWITZ

I would never take credit away from Cameron Boxer. He created the Positive Action Group, which was the greatest club in the history of Sycamore Middle School—maybe even in the history of middle school, period.

But Cam was such a laid-back guy. If it weren't for his accomplishments, I might have been tempted to say there were times he seemed like a slacker. And I couldn't help wondering if the P.A.G. might be even better with more of a "high-energy" person at the head.

Me, for instance.

The fund-raiser was a smash hit. We raised over $11,000 for the library. Not exactly enough for the new building, but a fantastic start. The turnout was triple what we expected, and business was so good that I gave the order—and Mr. Fanshaw agreed—to stay open for an extra hour.

In fact, the only thing that went wrong was when String's hamburger station ran out of hot mustard and people had to use the regular kind. As P.A.G. president, I had to take responsibility for that. I would definitely be better prepared next time.

Oh, yeah—there was also that part at the end where a riot broke out and all the tables got smashed.

Lucky for us, Dr. Casper, our town vet, was there, or it would have taken a lot longer than twenty minutes to get Elvis under control. Poor little soul; he was almost crazy. What did we expect with hundreds of people dozens of times his size trying to catch him? It was a miracle he didn't get stomped on. That would have been dangerous, especially since Elvis had lost so much weight. He looked more like a super-tall bucktoothed squirrel these days—except for the big flat tail. At least that wasn't going to waste away.

When Dr. Casper finally got his arms around Elvis, Chucky showed up with his pet carrier. That was why he was such a great boyfriend: In the middle of so much chaos, he had run all the way home and come back with exactly what we needed. A girl could depend on a guy like that.

Dr. Casper frowned at the cage. "That's okay for a cat or a small dog. But the door latch isn't strong enough to hold in a wild animal like a beaver."

"Tell me about it," put in Cam in a forlorn voice.

Considering the vet *had* just told him about it, that comment didn't make a lot of sense.

"But why did he come here?" I asked Dr. Casper. "A wild animal stays away from crowds of people, right?"

"Depends on the wild animal," Pavel interjected. "If you're a hungry lion, technically, crowds of people could be a big attraction."

Chucky and I had a very mature relationship. I wasn't so sure about the other two members of the so-called Awesome Threesome, though.

The vet seemed stumped. "Beavers are ordinarily very territorial. I don't know what made your Elvis wander so far from his lodge."

"I do," I said mournfully. "He isn't happy. Look how skinny he is."

"It's normal for a beaver to be underweight coming out of the winter," Dr. Casper assured me. "There are many reasons why a beaver might wander. Confusing smells might upend his sense of territory. Especially if he believes he's pursuing a mate—"

"A mate?" I jumped on that. "You mean, like, a *girlfriend*?"

The vet laughed. "It's just one of many possibilities. Try not to assign too many human characteristics to a wild animal. In the long run, his nature will tell him how to behave."

But the more I thought about it, the more logical it seemed. Chucky and I had found each other. Why not Elvis? He deserved happiness, too.

Could it be that Elvis sensed a girlfriend in the area somewhere? Maybe another beaver who got separated from her colony when they built the new mall across town?

Chucky wasn't a big fan of that theory. "I don't know, Daph," he said as the P.A.G. cleanup crew carried what was left of the smashed library tables and piled them by the curb for the trash to haul away. "It sounds a little far-fetched to me. Shouldn't there be a simpler explanation?"

"Like what?"

"Well, like maybe somebody brought him here?"

"Who brings a beaver to a fund-raiser?" I demanded. "He doesn't have any money!"

"Well, maybe— *Ow!*"

As Pavel and Cam marched past lugging a broken desk, one of the legs whacked Chucky in the back of the head. If I hadn't known they were best friends, I'd have sworn they did it on purpose.

The three squared off, and a kind of message flashed among them that I couldn't quite put my finger on.

Part of it was definitely jealousy. Chucky was the first of them to have a girlfriend, and the other two felt left behind.

As good as a relationship could be, it could throw other friendships out of balance. It was absolutely worth it, but it was still kind of sad.

Elvis was lucky to be a beaver. When he found his mate, things would be a lot less complicated.

CHAPTER NINE
KELLY HANNITY

The hardest teacher at Sycamore Middle School was Mr. Proothi. If you ended up in one of his social studies classes, you'd better be ready to work twenty-five hours a day. He was a tough grader, too. A B-minus from Proothi was the equivalent of 100 percent from everybody else. There was a rumor that he once gave someone an A and the poor kid dropped dead of shock right there in the classroom.

The only things scarier than Mr. Proothi himself were his assignments. The worst part was how he told you about them—like a torturer who really enjoyed his job.

"Who's Who in the American Revolution will make up seventy percent of your grade. Do the math, people. There's no way you can pass if you don't ace this project. And if you don't pass social studies, no high school next year. So if you take this lightly, make sure you're the kind of person who appreciates sweating in an un-air-conditioned summer school classroom . . ."

I hated him, of course—we all did—but I wasn't worried about passing. I was a great student, and social studies was my favorite subject. Things like history and politics interested me—I was student body copresident along with

Jordan. I was in greater danger of being the next A-induced heart attack than I was of sweltering in summer school.

But that was me. You could see faces turning green as the teacher went on and on about how demanding this was going to be, how we had to learn to budget our time or else, and how no late papers would be accepted.

A hand waved in the air. "Can I go to the bathroom?" asked Cam Boxer.

Mr. Proothi frowned. "Don't you think you should wait until I've finished giving you the details of this assignment? After all, your school career could depend on it."

"So I can go?" Cam persisted. Without waiting for an answer, he got up and ran out of the room.

I was worried about Cam. A lot of people were. He created the P.A.G., which was the best thing about Sycamore Middle School. If it weren't for the P.A.G., Jordan and I never would have agreed to call off the election and share the president's job. But it wasn't just us; it was everybody. String might never have gotten back on the football team. Xavier might still have been in trouble with the law. Elvis wouldn't have his habitat, and the whole town would have lost our main exit ramp from the interstate.

The P.A.G. made life better for all of us.

All of us except for Cam.

He put his whole heart into the organization. He gave and gave and gave, never thinking of himself. And eventually, he fell so far behind in his schoolwork that he was in danger of flunking out.

That was why he went to the bathroom just now. He knew he didn't have a prayer of doing well on Who's Who in the American Revolution. And he knew that a jerk like Proothi would never be understanding enough to cut him a break.

It made me really sad. Guilty, too—we were all so wrapped up in our own accomplishments through the P.A.G. that we never noticed that the guy who made it possible was sinking in quicksand.

I waited for Cam to come back to class, but he never did. He must have been really upset to disappear like that. So when Mr. Proothi was done giving us the assignment, I excused myself, grabbed my iPad, and went to search for Cam.

The halls were deserted in the middle of fourth period. I stationed myself outside the boys' room to wait for him. After a couple of minutes, Pavel and Chuck emerged, stuffing their phones into their pockets. I always wondered what a student leader like Cam had in common with a couple of video-game heads like them.

"Is Cam in the bathroom?" I whispered.

They hemmed and hawed like I'd asked them for the nuclear launch codes, and disappeared around the corner.

I was brave enough to knock on the door. "Cam, are you in there? It's me, Kelly."

The door opened a crack, and he peered out at me. He looked tentative, like Punxsutawney Phil on Groundhog Day. Proothi must have really freaked him out.

He didn't say anything, so I forged ahead. "I've got all the details on the assignment. I can email it to you, if you want."

The question seemed to throw him. "Okay," he said finally.

I typed the address he gave me into my iPad. "You know what? I've got a ton of notes on the whole American Revolution unit. I'll send you those, too. It'll really help when you're doing the Who's Who."

I expected him to say thanks. Instead, he took off down the hall, tossing a haunted look over his shoulder.

It was more proof that these school problems had him completely spooked.

Proothi was a tyrant, but he wasn't a liar. Who's Who in the American Revolution turned out to be a real nightmare. We had to identify and list the contributions of over a hundred different people from revolutionary times. I felt good about my decision to share my notes with Cam. Without my help, this assignment might have derailed any chance he had of passing the year.

A few days later, I approached him in class and asked if my notes had been helpful so far on the Who's Who.

He looked completely blank. "Notes?"

At first, I was mad. Didn't he appreciate what I was trying to do for him? To go by his reaction, he hadn't even bothered to open my email!

Before an angry retort could tumble out of my mouth, I understood what was really happening here: The hero who'd created the P.A.G. and transformed a whole town was too embarrassed and too proud to admit he was in over his head.

My eyes actually filled with tears. He was even more admirable than I'd thought. What character! What dignity!

It made me twice as determined as before to make sure he passed Proothi's torture test. But how could you help a guy who had too much grace to accept anybody's help?

Suddenly, I had the answer.

CHAPTER TEN
CAMERON BOXER

From space, the planet Geldorf was a peaceful blue-and-yellow orb—but don't you believe it.

As my ship slipped into orbit, deadly disruptor bolts from planetary defense blasted all around, vaporizing smaller vessels in my fleet. Fighter drones from the surface buzzed like fireflies, lighting up the darkness with lethal laser beams. A strontium torpedo went off like a miniature exploding sun, close enough to fry my starboard deflector shield. Damage reports filled my viewscreen. One more direct hit, and I was a goner.

In other words, it was ill.

Guardians of Geldorf was everything I remembered and more. How I survived for all these months without it was beyond me. And to find a replacement copy on sale for one dollar in the library's throwaway junk restored my faith in miracles.

Even though *Guardians* was an older game, it was super realistic. The controller vibrated in my hands as my shuttlecraft descended through the turbulence of the atmosphere to the alien surface. It was something I'd done hundreds of times before—you know, before Melody threw out our copy. But this was the first time I'd ever invaded Geldorf as a streamer, with hundreds of followers watching.

"Hang on!" I shouted into the headset, my voice garbled by the gummy worms in my cheeks. "It's going to be a bumpy ride!"

What a rush! My fingers moved at lightning speed over the controls. My concentration was 100 percent—even when I took a beaver tail in the side of the head.

Elvis loved *Guardians*, too. Oh, sure, he was just a beaver and shouldn't have been able to tell the difference. But you just knew from his reactions that he understood he was watching something special. He couldn't stay on the back of the couch. He was constantly leaping around—onto my shoulder, my lap, even the top of my head. And that weird crying-baby sound he sometimes made—it was practically nonstop today. His flat tail worked like a piston against the couch and me.

I swooped low over the aliens' power station, swerving to avoid two antiaircraft hover-grenades. My strategy was to knock out the power grid before the invasion force began to land. That way, the extraterrestrials' targeting systems would be offline.

"Time to turn out the lights," I announced, my finger floating over the button.

I hesitated. The target looked a little different than I

remembered it—probably because this was an earlier version of the game than I was used to. Some of my followers were noticing the same thing. A lot of the comments in my feed were asking about the actual copy of the game I was playing—how old it was, what year I'd bought it; one guy even wanted to know the serial number. Like I had time to check on that in the middle of a full-scale planetary invasion!

I launched the missile. The power station went up in a fireball. The planet went dark . . . and a car door slammed outside, close enough to make Elvis jump.

A few seconds later, I heard Melody's voice upstairs. "Hi, Dad—what are you doing home *so early*?"

Involuntarily, my jaw clenched, and the gummy worms cemented my teeth together. I barely managed to mumble, "Checking on the serial number," before taking GameFox229 offline.

Upstairs, Dad said, "I've got a killer headache. Mom volunteered to cover for me. Where's your brother?"

"You have to ask? He's in the basement."

The next thing I knew, there were footsteps on the stairs. I grabbed Elvis, but there was nowhere to hide him—and no time to do it. I watched helplessly as the figure came into view—Melody.

"Go around the back," I hissed urgently. "I'll get on a chair and hand Elvis out through the window."

"Are you kidding? I'm not touching that disgusting smell factory!"

"It's an emergency! You want Dad to catch us?"

"He'll catch *you*," she corrected. "It's not my problem. I'm not the star of GameFox229."

"It's twenty percent your problem," I snarled. "You took a cut of this, remember?"

"I took twenty percent of the good stuff," she informed me. "When we crash and burn, that's all you." And she disappeared up the stairs.

I was already on the phone to Chuck. The Awesome Threesome wouldn't let me down.

The next three minutes were the longest of my life. Finally, there was a tapping at the basement window. Weak with relief, I climbed onto the chair and handed Elvis out into the waiting arms of . . .

"Pavel?" I whispered. "I called Chuck."

He gathered the beaver into his arms. "Yeah, well, he couldn't make it. *Duckne* had plans."

"The nerve of that guy!"

Pavel shrugged. "At least he called me. Don't complain. He could have left you hanging."

I pushed the carrier out, too—a pretty tight squeeze. "I'll be there in a minute."

I cleaned up the newspapers, pulled off the Zorro mask, and headed upstairs. This had been a crummy afternoon, with me interrupting my stream and all that. I'd definitely lose some followers, which wasn't good.

But in another way, it was a positive development. Dad came home in the middle of everything, Melody left me twisting in the wind, Chuck let me down, and we still survived. And now we had a disaster plan in case any bad things happened in the future.

Dad was at the kitchen sink, drinking some Tylenol.

"Whoa!" He stopped me as I made for the back door. "Listen, Cam, I know that's your man cave down there, but you're starting to stink like a barn. Take a shower, will you?"

"I will," I promised, and ran out to join Pavel.

By that time, he had managed to coax Elvis into the carrier. We doubled-sealed the gate with a square of duct tape—thank you, Dr. Casper—and got on our bikes to haul the little guy home.

"Thanks, man," I told Pavel as we pedaled for the woods, the cage on my handlebars. "You were a lifesaver back there. Not like 'Chucky.' You know, this whole boyfriend thing is starting to get on my nerves."

"Starting?" Pavel echoed. "Where have you been, Cam—Alpha Centauri? When's the last time three words came out of that kid's mouth without two of them being 'Daphne thinks' or 'Daphne says'?"

"I guess I've been distracted with my stream lately," I admitted.

"Sure." Pavel was bitter. "You've got your lifestyle. Chuck's got Daphne. The Awesome Threesome is down to just me, and technically it's not so awesome anymore. Even Mrs. Backward noticed. She said: 'Alone you are today?'"

"It'll get better," I promised. "Once GameFox229 is more established, it won't take up so much of my time. And Chuck is bound to come to his senses sooner or later."

"Really?" Pavel was unconvinced. "He took so many pictures of his precious Daphne that he ran out of memory on his phone. So to free up space, he deleted *games*."

I swerved and almost flung Elvis into the ditch, pet carrier and all. "This boyfriend thing is like a disease."

Pavel nodded sadly. "And our friend's got a bad case of it. The worst part is we can't even tell Chuck what a dope he's being. He'll just say we're jealous, or we're too immature to understand what it's like to be part of a ship."

When a smart guy like Pavel didn't know what to do about a problem, you could be sure you were up against something really tough. Okay, GameFox229 was my top priority, but the Awesome Threesome was important, too. I'd always assumed that Pavel, Chuck, and I would be friends forever. But when a guy started deleting games from his phone, the whole world was out of whack.

Elvis seemed happy enough to be back in his habitat, although he did glance around in confusion, like he was trying to locate the TV. *Guardians of Geldorf* did that to a person—or even a beaver, I guess.

Pavel and I were going to hit Sweetness and Light, but then I remembered Who's Who in the American Revolution was due tomorrow, and I hadn't even started yet.

"For Proothi?" Pavel was wide-eyed. "You're dead, man. I did it last semester. It's the toughest assignment all year."

"No biggie." I shrugged. "Somebody sent me some notes last week. I forget who. And I forget why. But it's definitely about the What's What."

"Who's Who," he corrected.

"Whatever."

As I pedaled home, I reflected that I should just take a zero from Proothi. That way, when everybody thought I was flunking, it would be the truth. But that wouldn't go over too well with the parental units. If they took away my console, sayonara, GameFox229. So much for honesty being the best policy.

At the house, I headed down to the basement. My computer was part of the streaming setup, but I occasionally used it for homework when it was absolutely unavoidable. I checked my email inbox, which was mostly full of reminders from gaming sites about how many points/coins/tokens/dollars/stars/crowns/trophies/smiley faces/shekels/yen I'd earned. There it was—*Hannity, Kelly.* With her notes, I should be able to knock this out in no time.

I opened the email and my eyes fell on the list of historical figures I had to research. My heart sank as I scrolled through the long list of names. Yikes, I didn't know there were this many people in all of history, much less one little revolution. Eleven pages! If I had to research everybody here, I wouldn't be done till the *next* revolution!

I thought hard, trying to remember if Mr. Proothi had told us a shortcut on how to research so many names. But all I could dredge up were worthless bits of advice like *Budget your time* and *Don't even think about trying to knock it out in one night.* Wasn't that just like a teacher? What if one night was all you had left?

Then I saw it. There was a second email from Kelly in my inbox. At first I thought it was just a duplicate of the notes, but then I realized that it had come several days later. There was no subject line and no message, just a document. Intrigued, I double-clicked on it.

It was the same list of historical figures as before. Only—I goggled—each name came with a paragraph that explained who each person was, and why he or she was important in the American Revolution.

It hit me: This wasn't *notes* on the *Who's Who*; this was the finished assignment—signed, sealed, and delivered!

I was amazed. Why would Kelly send me her work? Why would anybody? It didn't make sense. Unless . . .

Kelly already sent me the notes once. What if she tried to do it again—a backup, just in case the first email never made it to me? But instead of just notes, she attached the whole project—her own.

I switched back and forth between the two emails from *Hannity, Kelly.* First the notes, eleven pages of names. Days of research—days I didn't have. Second, the completed project. Zero research, because everything had already been done. All that remained was to submit it to Proothi on the school's turn-it-in site. Thirty seconds, tops.

I took a gummy worm from the bowl and chewed thoughtfully. That would be wrong. Wrong to take advantage of Kelly's mistake. Wrong to hand in somebody else's work as my own.

On the other hand, Kelly wanted to help me pass. She even said so. That was why she'd sent me her notes on the Who's Who in the first place.

I clicked back to the first email. If I started from here, I'd never finish in time, not even if I pulled an all-nighter. I'd flunk, which would be like a slap in the face to Kelly, who was trying to give me a break. But . . .

I clicked on the finished Who's Who. If I took Kelly's

project, rearranged the order, changed the font, and switched a few words around—you know, *hard* to *difficult*, etc.—then I'd pass with flying colors. That would make everybody happy—Kelly, Mr. Proothi, and definitely me. It would even be good for Elvis, since GameFox229 would continue, and the little guy was turning into my biggest fan.

The more I thought about it, the more it seemed like a great deal for everybody. I wouldn't be not doing work. I'd be doing a different kind of work, since I'd use the extra time for streaming—work that would bring me closer to 50,000 subscribers.

I copied the document, made the changes, and converted the whole thing into Old English script—very classy. At the last minute, I remembered to delete the part where it said *By Kelly Hannity* and stuck my own name in there. That would have been a dead giveaway.

"For GameFox," I breathed aloud, and hit upload.

The beauty of these turn-it-in sites was that it was already in Proothi's inbox. All over in a heartbeat—no regrets, no looking back.

Gamer heaven.

CHAPTER ELEVEN
MR. FANSHAW

When Cameron Boxer had been running the Positive Action Group, I couldn't quite escape the feeling that something was off.

Don't get me wrong—a public service club like the P.A.G. was every guidance counselor's dream. There I was, buried under a mountain of unsold raffle tickets when Cameron came along and changed everything. Suddenly, short-sighted, self-centered middle schoolers came forward to volunteer to give up their free time, even their weekends, for the good of the community. Our only problem was that our numbers grew so fast that we had too many volunteers and not enough projects for them to help with.

There was never any question that Cameron made it happen, yet he always seemed removed from it all, like it had nothing to do with him, and he was just some stranger who had wandered into a party by mistake. It defied understanding. On the one hand, he was the greatest student leader I'd ever worked with. On the other, I never really worked with him. Most of the time, I couldn't even find him. When the office paged him, he didn't come. Staking out his locker didn't help—he had others around the building so he could avoid you. When the bell rang at three thirty, he was out of the school and gone in a puff of smoke. Most of the time I had to stalk him outside the boys' room when I needed to discuss something P.A.G.-related.

I use the word *discuss* very loosely here. I did the talking while he scanned the hall for an escape route. To have a conversation with Cameron meant you had to supply both sides. And the inevitable takeaway was that this boy knew absolutely nothing about the club he'd founded—and he didn't want to know. The only evidence to the contrary was the P.A.G. itself. It was a huge success, a town legend, and had attracted virtually every student in the entire school.

I never thought I'd miss those days, slinking through the halls, trying to find Cameron and pin him down. Now Cameron had stepped back from the Positive Action Group, but I was still slinking. I was hiding from the acting president of the P.A.G., Daphne Leibowitz.

Unlike Cameron, Daphne was exactly what you'd expect a student leader to be—motivated, outspoken, high-energy, ambitious, and bold times twenty. She was determined to make the P.A.G. her whole life—and mine. With Cameron, I had to do all the talking; with Daphne, I was lucky to get three words in to her five hundred.

On Wednesday, she stormed into my office and slammed an envelope down on my desk.

"What's this?" I asked, hating myself for asking.

"Open it!" she urged.

Inside was a second envelope, folded into thirds. When I got into that one, I pulled out—

"A tea bag?" I asked, holding it by the string.

"Don't you get it? It's a do-it-yourself tea party. We print the school's address on the inner envelope, and everybody puts in their donations."

I was mystified. "But where's the tea party?"

"That's what makes it do-it-yourself," she explained. "You make your own tea in your own house, and the P.A.G. gets money for it. It's a great fund-raiser for the library!"

"We can't do that, Daphne," I told her. "Too much postage. If we don't get enough donations, we'll lose money on the deal."

Daphne had an answer for that. "You don't need postage when you've got people power. We'll send paggers to deliver to every house in town. And they'll go back a few days later to pick up the donations."

I had a vision of kids going door to door, shaking down citizens for their do-it-yourself tea. "No, Daphne. It's a good idea, but it just won't work."

"Okay," she said brightly. "I'll think of something else."

I didn't doubt it for a nanosecond. Daphne always thought of something else. She thought of a lot of somethings. She proposed using school property to host a massive three-day carnival; she suggested we cancel classes for a week and hire eighth graders out as temporary farm laborers; she wanted students to bid on having their teachers locked in a cell for an hour at our municipal jail; she even floated a plan to set up a toll booth on Main Street and actually charge people a dollar for the privilege of driving across town.

Sometimes Daphne brought Chuck Kinsey with her on these missions to pepper me with fund-raising ideas. The two of them were going out, "shipping," or whatever middle schoolers called it these days. Chuck seemed to be part of Cameron's inner circle, along with Pavel Dysan, one of our academic superstars. Between Pavel's smarts and Cameron's success as a student leader, Chuck seemed like the odd man out. He had Daphne—that was a kind of claim to fame.

If Chuck was there to lend credibility to her suggestions, it wasn't working. Most of the time, he seemed even more overwhelmed by her than I was—and that was saying something.

It got to the point where I started hanging out in colleagues' offices during class change or whenever Daphne had lunch or a free period. It was a little awkward, especially when they asked me what I was doing there. What was I supposed to tell them—that I lived in fear of one of my own students?

The irony wasn't lost on me. I was hiding from Daphne the way Cameron used to hide from me. Well, not exactly, because Daphne always managed to find me anyway.

She tracked me down as I made my break from the cafeteria line to the faculty dining lounge.

"Mr. Fanshaw!"

Out of the corner of my eye, I spotted her familiar power walk behind me—shoulders back, arms swinging.

I pretended not to hear her in the noisy cafeteria. I quickened my pace. My tomato soup began to spill all over my chocolate nut brownie, but it was worth it. The lounge was only a few yards away, and it was private—a Daphne-free zone.

"Mr. Fanshaw!" She took hold of my wrist and wheeled me around.

I lost it the way no guidance counselor ever should. "No, Daphne, I won't authorize you to set up an illegal toll booth to shake down innocent motorists for the greater glory of the Sycamore Library!"

Her eager face crumpled, and I was instantly contrite. "I'm sorry. I shouldn't have snapped at you. It's just that—I was really looking forward to that brownie." I gazed down at my dessert. It looked like it had been murdered, sodden and ruined in a pool of bloodred soup.

"I wasn't going to ask about that," she said in a hurt tone. "I read about this school on the Internet. They sold cookie dough to raise money—"

"I'll think it over," I soothed.

"I'm under a lot of stress," she complained. "All those paggers—they keep asking what the next P.A.G. project is going to be. They'd never go to Cam. He's too focused on schoolwork."

I'd heard this rumor among the kids—that the reason Cameron was taking a break from the P.A.G. was that he was struggling in his classes and wanted to bring up his academics before refocusing on the club. It was a bit of a head-scratcher. I checked his report cards, and his current grades were about what they'd always been—not spectacular by any means, but certainly not failing. If anything, they were on the way up. He'd just gotten an A on Mr. Proothi's Who's Who in the American Revolution, and that was generally considered one of the toughest assignments in the whole school.

"Don't be so hard on yourself," I advised gently. "Everyone agrees you're doing a wonderful job with the P.A.G."

"It's not just the P.A.G.," she insisted. "It's Elvis."

"What's wrong with Elvis?" I probed.

"Unrequited love."

She held up her hand to silence my protest. "I know it sounds crazy, but Dr. Casper backs me up."

"The veterinarian?"

"He says one of the reasons a beaver might wander is he senses the presence of a mate," she reasoned. "Well, Elvis wanders *all* the time now. He's almost never in his habitat. And he still hasn't put on the weight he lost over the winter. He's unsettled! He needs to find a girlfriend and bring her back to the lodge to start a family!"

I truly, honestly, had no idea what to say to all that. It hadn't come up—not even once—during my professional training as a guidance counselor.

I still considered the Positive Action Group the greatest achievement of my career. But all too often lately, it felt like trying to enjoy a brownie that had soaked up too much tomato soup.

CHAPTER TWELVE
CAMERON BOXER

I never had much use for email—except to get activation codes for gaming sites. But lately, it was becoming a big part of my life.

Today when I checked my inbox, there were eleven new messages—and only ten of them were ads for diet pills and cures for baldness. The other was from Jordan, and when I opened it, a long list of numbers appeared on my computer screen.

I almost called Jordan to ask about it, but I couldn't spare the time. Elvis and I had a really long session as GameFox229 after school, and then I had to clean up and bike him back to his habitat. There was no question about it—the beaver was more into *Guardians* than any of the other games we'd played. And my followers felt the same way. Every session, my numbers climbed higher—well over a thousand, these days. If this kept up, I would have to focus on *Guardians* only. Streaming was entertainment; I had to give the people what they wanted.

"Are you getting enough sleep?" my mother demanded at dinner. "You look like you're about to doze off in the spaghetti sauce."

I straightened up and Melody snickered.

"Hey!" I snapped at her. "I have the right to be tired. I'm working hard . . ."

My voice trailed off. Melody, of all people, knew exactly what I was working hard at. She even owned 20 percent of it.

"That's the go-getter I always knew you could be," Dad approved, slurping a noodle. "There's more to life than video games."

I let that pass, even when my sister kicked me under the table.

After dinner, I had homework to do, which made things even worse. What a week for Miss Glickman to hand out a ninety-question review sheet in algebra! I mean, no week would be good for that much math, but this was an extra-bad time for it.

I went upstairs and got to work, which felt like when your console crashes and you have to restart all your games at Level 1. And then a funny thing happened. As I struggled along, the numbers started to look *familiar*.

How could that be? Had I done this review before? It didn't make sense. Sure, I was distracted, but I wasn't crazy. This was definitely not the kind of torture a guy could ever forget.

I struggled through another couple of questions. Same situation. I *knew* these answers; it felt as if I'd just seen them!

Then it came to me. I took out my phone and opened Jordan's email. The long list of numbers appeared on the small screen. And the top six were a perfect match for the first six answers of my homework!

I scrolled down the message. Ninety numbers; ninety questions on the review sheet. Jordan had sent me the entire assignment. Why would he do that?

The answer was obvious: For the same reason Kelly had given me her Who's Who. At first, I'd thought Kelly had attached the wrong file—the finished product instead of the notes. But there was no way Jordan's was a mistake.

They'd both done it to help me raise my "failing" grades.

I'd painted the picture of the floundering P.A.G. president. But I'd only done that so people would leave me alone. I'd never said anything about doing my work for me!

It was wrong. All wrong. Completely wrong. Not that I was a big homework fan, but this couldn't be allowed to go on. I had to tell Kelly and Jordan to cut it out.

But first, I had a math assignment to finish. Let me tell you, it wasn't easy to sweat over a problem when the answer was right there on your phone, eight inches from your pencil hand.

Confession: I peeked—just to confirm that I had number seven right. Nothing wrong with that. But while I was checking, I saw the solution to eight. And what was I going to do? Not use it?

After that, the dam burst. It seemed so pointless to beat my brains out till midnight when I already had the answers. I copied them all, examples nine through ninety. I wasn't proud of it, but I wasn't exactly ashamed, either. Hey, I'd finished eight of them on my own—okay, seven—so it wasn't like I didn't know how to do the work. And anyway, education was supposed to make you smarter. How smart was a guy who would work his fingers to the bone when there was a much easier way to get the job done?

Besides, I was going to put a stop to this first thing in the morning. I'd talk to Kelly and Jordan and tell them thanks but no thanks.

When I arrived at school the next day, my locker had been tampered with. The combination lock hung open and I knew for a fact that I had closed it yesterday. The thing is, this was not my official locker—I had three others around the building, strategically located near exits. If Mr. Fandoodle wanted to waste any more of my precious streaming time, he'd have to catch me first.

So I had two things to worry about: 1) Who had broken into my locker? and 2) How did this person know it was my locker in the first place?

I eased the door open and peered inside.

Everything looked normal. There were a few books, a fleece I didn't wear anymore because the zipper was broken, and a gross black thing that might once have been a banana. Taped to the wall was a yellowed piece of paper with passwords to gaming sites and—what was this?

My project for art class. It was supposed to be a picture of our house, but it got real blobby because the watercolors were too wet. It wasn't my fault. Why would they call them watercolors if there wasn't supposed to be water? And the more I tried to fix it, the more it looked like soppy oatmeal. My Plan B was to change the name from *Our House* to *Clouds*, because I didn't think I'd get away with calling it *Oatmeal*.

It was different now. There were flecks of blue and white in the oatmeal. It was water—a lake reflecting bright sun. And a sailboat in the distance, not detailed, but really well drawn. You could almost sense it moving toward you.

It was the Who's Who and the math assignment all over again. Somebody had broken into my secret locker and fixed my painting.

My mind raced. It had to be a pagger who was close enough to me to know about my extra lockers, who was a good artist, and who had burglary skills.

"Don't worry about the lock," rumbled a deep voice behind me. "It's not broken."

I wheeled to find myself face-to-pecs with Xavier. I tilted my head enough to see him looking down at me.

He inclined his giant head toward the picture. "What do you think?"

"It's—it's—too good," I replied.

"Thanks," he said.

"I don't know if I can hand it in."

His flinty eyes narrowed. "Why not?"

Why not? Because it was a picture of a boat on a lake, and I'd painted everything except the boat and the lake. My only contribution was the oatmeal. It was as much my work as the math review and the Who's Who.

But Xavier was so anxious to please, so earnest, so sincere . . . and so *big*. Did I have the guts to tell this giant that his hard work on my behalf was unwanted?

Not on my life.

"It's just that—I've never painted anything this good before."

He shrugged a massive pair of shoulders. "So you improved."

"I improved." I gulped.

Okay, maybe Xavier wasn't the best place to start to make my stand about people doing my schoolwork for me. I would still talk to Kelly and Jordan. They were a lot less scary than Xavier.

"I heard Proothi gave you an A on the Who's Who," Kelly told me with a wink. "Me too."

"Yeah, thanks and all that," I said. "But from now on—you know, going forward—"

She snapped her fingers. "You mean the end-of-the-unit test. Say no more."

"But what I mean is—"

She cut me off. "Don't worry, I'll put together a study guide and get it to you ASAP."

It went even worse with Jordan. He just flashed me a thumbs-up, like we had planned the whole thing together.

And the emails kept coming. I thought one of them was spam, but then I recognized the paragraph I had to write for Spanish. The sender was this kid Brittany Cruz, who didn't even take Spanish. She just spoke it. So what must have happened was somebody in my class told Brittany I needed help, and Brittany provided it.

I barely knew this girl. I had no idea where to go to find her. I wasn't even sure I remembered what she looked like. And before I could ask anybody, a new message pinged in, this one from *McBean, Freeland*. It was the weirdest of all. It looked like an X-ray of somebody's foot.

"It's The String's MRI from when I had my high ankle sprain back in seventh grade," String told me when I asked about it. "Hard times, man. I was only slightly faster than everybody else."

"It's . . . great," I managed. "But why did you send it to me?"

"You've got DiPasquale for health, right? The sports medicine unit should be starting any day now. You can write a paper on this. See how the soft tissue is swollen, but the bone is okay? Nobody gets injured like The String."

By the end of lunch, there were three more messages in my inbox. I didn't even open them, but I knew exactly what they were.

There was only one thing for me to do: Delete. All of it. Everything. Right after school.

During eighth period, Mr. DiPasquale announced, "Sports are such a huge part of our culture today, so it's important for us to study the health implications of athletics. So you might want to start thinking about a topic for your term project on sports medicine."

I already knew what my topic was going to be. I had an MRI of it on my phone.

That night, I pasted Brittany's Spanish paragraph into Google Translate. If I was going to hand it in, I should at least know what it said.

CHAPTER THIRTEEN
CHUCK KINSEY

Being in a relationship was a lot more complicated than I thought it would be.

Like when your girlfriend was upset about something and you had information that would put her mind at rest. You couldn't tell her without betraying your two best friends. But how could you stand around and let her suffer?

I knew Elvis wasn't away from his habitat because he was out searching for a girlfriend. Elvis was away from his habitat because he was in Cam Boxer's basement!

"Daphne's driving herself crazy worrying about where Elvis goes every day," I argued over gummy worms at Sweetness and Light. "She's terrified he's going to get run over while he's out looking for this mate who doesn't exist. We have to tell her the truth."

Cam waved an extra-long worm in my face. "Are you nuts? She'd have a fit!"

"Maybe," I agreed. "But then we'd bring her to your place to see how much Elvis loves video games. I think he likes it more than anything else he does."

"He doesn't do anything else," Pavel pointed out. "He's a beaver. What are his hobbies? Stamp collecting? Mixed martial arts?"

"Still," I insisted, "Daphne is only interested in Elvis's happiness. Sure, she may be a little weirded out by the streaming part at first—"

"She'd never accept it," Pavel cut me off. "She'd accuse Cam of exploiting an innocent animal. She might even blame him for Elvis being skinny."

"And how can we be sure that's not true?" I shot back.

It brought hoots of outrage from my two best friends.

Mrs. Backward stepped out from behind the candy counter. "Fighting, you boys are," she announced.

"Technically, we're just speaking with emphasis," Pavel corrected.

She looked disapprovingly at the full bowl in front of Cam. "Your appetite, you lost?"

"I'm not really feeling gummy worms today," Cam admitted. "I'll take these to go."

She scowled. "My best customer, I can't afford to lose. A living, I'm trying to make."

Cam really was her best customer these days—even better than Pavel and me. The whole GameFox229 setup required gummy worms so he could disguise his voice. He went through a ton of them every streaming session. Maybe that was why he wasn't hungry for them now.

When you have to eat them for business, it makes it less fun in your free time.

The storekeeper returned to the cash register, and I explained further. "I agree with you—Elvis likes video games. But that's definitely not normal for a beaver. They're supposed to swim and chew wood, not hang out in some kid's basement. How can we be sure that isn't what's keeping him skinny? Maybe changing his routine messed up his eating habits. You eat less, you lose weight."

"Skinny," Cam repeated. "You make it sound like that's a bad thing. Why don't you say that he's non-overweight? And anyway, even if Daphne was cool about Elvis in my basement, we still couldn't tell her. As far as all those paggers know, I'm studying, not streaming. GameFox229 has to stay secret."

I was bitter. "So I have to risk my love life for your streaming! How come you don't have to risk your streaming for my love life?"

"Hey!" Pavel exclaimed. "We were the Awesome Threesome long before there was ever a good ship Duckne. Technically, the one who changed everything is *you*."

I stared at Pavel. "What are you saying?"

He spread his arms wide. "We used to get together after school every day. Now maybe we see you, maybe we don't. It all depends on *Daphne*. We used to team up for every online game. But it stinks to be teammates with someone you can't rely on because he's always got plans with his girlfriend. Listen to yourself, man. It's all *Daphne* this and *Daphne* that. Like Chuck disappeared and this representative of Duckne showed up in his place."

I was stunned. "I thought you guys would be happy for me when I got a girlfriend."

"There you go again," Pavel accused. "*Your* girlfriend. *Your* life. You, you, you." He picked up a gummy worm, stared at it, and threw it down on the table. "This whole thing is turning my stomach." He stormed out of Sweetness and Light.

Mrs. Backward looked as if she wanted to mix in, but thought better of it. "My own business, I mind," she announced.

It was a strange time for the Awesome Threesome. We were definitely still together, because Pavel and I were both friends with Cam. But we weren't really friends with each other anymore. At least not in the old way.

On the surface, everything was fine. Better than fine. Pavel stopped giving me a hard time about Daphne. And when Daphne herself was around he was extra nice to her—even to the point where she started to notice.

"You know, Pavel's turning into a really good guy. I used to think he didn't like me very much."

"Where'd you get that idea?" I managed to choke.

I almost hated the niceness worse than the fighting. It wasn't the real Pavel, and he and I both knew it.

In spite of everything, we were stuck together. We were in a lot of the same classes at school. Our lockers were right next to each other. And we were helping Cam with GameFox229. It was uncomfortable and kind of sad.

Our friendship may have been circling the bowl, but GameFox229 was taking off like a rocket. It seemed like every day Cam added hundreds of viewers to his online following. By that weekend, he was up over 2,000, and the flood of comments was moving so fast that Pavel or I had to monitor it on a separate iPad. We'd choose the best questions and write them on a whiteboard so we could hold them up for Cam to read and answer as he gamed.

Better than that, Cam was starting to pick up *subscribers*. Subscribers were more important than regular followers because they actually paid money to be premium members of the stream. It was subscribers who made it possible for streaming to be a guy's real job. Cam hardly ever shut up about the magical number of 50,000. He wasn't anywhere close to that yet, but he was on his way.

Why was GameFox229 becoming so famous? Well, for one thing, Cam was getting comfortable in the Zorro mask, and speaking a lot more clearly with the gummy worms in his cheeks. Plus, he was playing *Guardians* full-time now, and he was really good at it. He screamed his head off while battling the Geldorfian defenders, who were all insects, but a lot bigger. Plus he had Elvis, who was pretty unique. There were no other beavers in streaming, even if there were a lot of them in streams.

Still, the biggest attraction turned out to be the game itself. It was hard to figure out why. *Guardians* had been around for years. There must have been millions of copies floating around. *I* owned one. So did Pavel. I bet at least a hundred other kids in our school did, too.

But because Cam had an older copy of the game, there seemed to be certain details that looked a little different, and Cam's followers were obsessed with them. You could see it in the scrolling comment feed: *Why is the Hive Dome bluish instead of silvery gray? Some of the arachnids only have six legs when they should have eight. The praying mantises' thoraxes are the wrong shape. The Honeycomb of Eternal Pollination isn't shiny enough. Does that mean it isn't radioactive?* There were endless queries about the copyright date on the game box, and where Cam had gotten it. And this question—most confusing of all:

When will you reach Level 13???

Cam laughed. "It's a joke. Everybody knows *Guardians* is a twelve-level game."

One night, as I was drifting off to sleep, my phone started going crazy on my nightstand, buzzing and vibrating across the tabletop.

At first I thought it might be Daphne, getting in the last good night of the day. But it was a Skype from Cam.

"What's up?" I asked warily.

He was all business. "I'm conferencing in Pavel."

"Pavel?" I seriously doubted he wanted to talk to me, and I knew for a fact that I wasn't too thrilled about talking to him.

But when Pavel's face appeared on the split screen, his eyes were wide.

"What's going on?" I demanded impatiently.

"Guys, I've been doing some research." His voice was hoarse with excitement. "Level Thirteen—it's real!"

CHAPTER FOURTEEN
CAMERON BOXER

It was the illest thing I'd ever heard.

It turned out the copy of *Guardians* I'd bought at the fund-raiser didn't just *look* a little different. It was a totally different game!

Pavel dug up the whole story on the Internet. When *Guardians of Geldorf* was first released, it had *thirteen* levels, not twelve. But that original version got banned in forty-seven states because of "inappropriate content" in Level 13. The outcry was so huge that the company pulled every single copy of the game off the market.

Or at least they thought they did. They could never be sure they'd found them all. A few units of the original had to be out there somewhere. And one of them had been tucked away in a corner of the old Sycamore Public Library—the one I'd snagged for a buck that Saturday.

So now gamers from all over the Internet were flocking to GameFox229. They liked my streaming; they liked my beaver. But mostly they were coming for a chance to catch a glimpse of the forbidden Level 13.

"I wonder what's so bad about it?" Chuck mused when

we met before school the next morning. "What could be awful enough to get banned in forty-seven states?"

I shrugged. "Probably just violence. You know how adults think. If anything's cool, it must be bad for people."

"I don't know," Pavel put in. "Skulls get bashed in, buildings blow up, zombies rip people to pieces, and those games never get outlawed. What do you have to do to be considered technically 'inappropriate'?"

"What if Level Thirteen is so gross that everyone who plays it barfs?" Chuck suggested timidly.

I thought it over. "Newbies, maybe. Any experienced gamer is used to a lot of blood and guts."

"Or it could be really scary," Chuck went on in growing agitation. "Like some guy got so freaked out he had a stroke with the controller still in his hands. That might make forty-seven states ban a game."

"I guess we're going to find out." Pavel turned to me. "You *are* going for Level Thirteen, right?"

"Are you kidding?" I crowed. "This is the best thing that could have happened! When word gets around that I've got the rare version of *Guardians*, the whole world is going to follow GameFox229. My fifty thousand subscribers are practically in the bag!"

Chuck was appalled. "Aren't you forgetting something? *Banned* means *against the law*."

"Banned in forty-seven states," I reminded him. "That means there are three states where it's totally okay."

"Yeah, but which ones?" Chuck persisted.

"That never came up in my research," Pavel admitted. "And there's another problem: Making it to Level Thirteen might not be as simple as you think. From what I read, Level Twelve is almost impossible to complete."

"Hey!" I said, insulted. "This is me you're talking about! I must have beaten that whole game a hundred times."

"You beat the *new* game," Pavel amended. "When they took out Thirteen, they made Twelve easier, too. But the original *Guardians* was one of the hardest games in history. Only a handful of people have ever seen Level Thirteen—and that was before you could stream or record your play to prove where you'd been. So for all we know, half of them are lying. Even Draja Dubrovnik never made it to Level Thirteen."

"No!" Chuck and I chorused.

Draja Dubrovnik was my all-time hero. Just his name sent shivers down my spine. There wasn't a record he couldn't shatter, a battle he couldn't dominate, a clan he couldn't lead, or an ultra-rare Pokémon he couldn't sniff out. He once crashed an entire network of online servers by earning so many coins that the computers couldn't keep track of them all. At eSports tournaments, the sight of his four-hundred-pound bulk lumbering onto the exhibit floor was enough to send challengers scurrying for the exits. With Draja around, the best anybody else could hope for would be second place. He'd dropped off the scene in recent years, but most people still considered him the greatest gamer ever.

"Bite your tongue," I said sharply. "Draja Dubrovnik could eat Level Thirteen for breakfast."

Pavel shook his head. "I read his interview in *Joystick* magazine. He admitted that the original *Guardians* was the only game he'd never been able to beat."

As we entered the school building, it all began to sink in. Here I was, standing on the doorstep of my life's ambition. My goal of 50,000 subscribers seemed so close that I could almost reach out and snag it with a Poké Ball.

But to achieve that, I was going to have to accomplish something that not even a titan of gaming had been able to do.

That night, I gave it a shot. Not on GameFox229—I wasn't ready for that yet. I didn't dare make the push for Level 13 until I knew how to complete 12. If Draja couldn't do it, it was going to be beyond hard. Fate—and the Sycamore Library—had handed me a golden opportunity to bust out as a major streamer. But I might throw that away if I failed online in front of my followers and looked like a newbie who'd never held a controller before.

So I was kicking it old school—no GameFox229, no beaver. Just me and a planetary defense force of hostile Geldorfians, man-to-insect, face-to-feeler.

It was nice to be playing without the Zorro mask, which was tight and kind of sweaty. And the absence of beaver smell was a definite upgrade. I also really loved not having to narrate—especially with my cheeks packed with candy. If I never tasted another gummy worm, it would be too soon for me.

Everything changed, though, when I got up past Level 10. The Geldorfians were fighting *back*. I mean, they fought back in my old game, too, but they had different weapons here. Better ones—stuff I swear I'd never seen before. A centurion who resembled a katydid waved something that looked like a pop-up toaster, and the next thing I knew, my laser melted, my shields were Play-Doh, and some kind of high-energy plasma blasted me all the way down to Level 6. I fought my way back okay, but this time my path was blocked by this giant millipede. He was unarmed, but he had plenty of legs, and he used sixty or seventy of them to kick my butt.

I was stunned. This wasn't the *Guardians* that I knew and loved. It was as if my favorite game had gone over to the dark side!

But any true gamer craved a challenge. I slogged my way through a swamp of pure liquid plutonium and made it to Level 12. There I stood outside the Hive Dome, gasping for breath while glowing radioactive slime oozed down my space suit.

That was when the plutonium hit the fan.

At first, I thought the game was broken, because I couldn't make out anything on the screen—just swirling chaos. Then I realized that the swirling was actually hundreds of tiny winged aliens, and they all were dive-bombing me. Every time I took a hit, the controller buzzed in my hands until it felt like one of those vibrating massage chairs you put money in at the mall.

I tried everything. I shot them. I blew them up with hover grenades. I used my portable wormhole and sucked them through to another dimension. I even swatted at them with a rolled-up newspaper. And still they kept coming until the swarm was so dense that I could barely move. As I watched my character fall to his knees under the weight of them, I pictured Draja Dubrovnik, great as he was, giving in to this overwhelming force. If he couldn't survive it, what hope was there for me?

The frustration poured out in a cry that began in my heart and worked its way up my throat and out my mouth.

"Cam?" called a voice from upstairs.

It was Melody. "Go away!" I snarled.

She descended the steps and came to stand beside the couch.

I paused the game, and she regarded the image on the screen. "Is that *Guardians*? I beat every level, but I don't remember this."

"It's an earlier version. I picked it up at the fund-raiser because some *idiot* lost our copy."

"Whatever." She was carrying her iPad and she opened the cover. "Listen, I think I got an email that was meant for you. Our addresses are close—*BoxerM* instead of *BoxerC*."

"Who from?" I asked without much interest. The game was still bugging me, and it bugged me even more that Melody could see I was getting annihilated.

"Joseph Ryerson," she replied, opening the message. "Funny thing—it looks like notes on a science experiment. Observations, measurements, even a conclusion. Why would he send you that? You barely know the kid."

In an instant, the danger facing my character in the game was replaced by the more serious danger confronting me in real life. The last thing I needed was for Melody to find out that helpful paggers were doing my schoolwork for me. She'd blackmail me till the end of time. And if she ever spilled the beans to Mom and Dad . . .

"Of course I know Joe," I told her. "We're pretty good friends. We did the experiment together."

She beamed at me. "That makes sense. Except—"

"Except what?"

"Except nobody calls him Joe. His name is Joseph James, and he goes by J.J. If you were really his friend, you'd probably know that, wouldn't you?"

CHAPTER FIFTEEN
MELODY BOXER

Whenever I complained about my brother, my parents' answer was always the same: "Don't be jealous!"

I was sick of hearing it. But they were right. I *was* jealous of Cam—only not because of the little-sister competitiveness they were accusing me of.

My brother was so *lucky*! I worked really hard for everything I had. Not Cam. Things dropped into his lap like manna from heaven. If he fell into a garbage dumpster, he'd come up with a gold watch. He invented a fake club to keep Mom and Dad from banning him from video games. Presto, the P.A.G. was born. He tried his hand at streaming because just *playing* video games twenty-four seven wasn't enough. Presto, thousands of followers beat a path to his door.

That was bad enough, but this latest thing beat it, hands down. People were doing his schoolwork for him. What other explanation could there be for someone he didn't even know sending him an entire science experiment?

My sleazy brother spread the word that he was failing in school because of all the hours he was putting into the P.A.G.—a number that was actually zero, by the way. Now the whole school had turned into his personal homework fairies. It proved what I always said: The P.A.G. may have been a great thing, but a lot of its members had nothing in their heads but air.

Sigh.

Of course, I could rat Cam out to Mom and Dad. Not even they could put a positive spin on what he was doing this time. They bit on the P.A.G. scam hook, line, and sinker, but there was no way to whitewash this. Tricking others into doing your work for you is cheating, pure and simple. Mom and Dad would have no choice but to see what a con man their son was turning into.

Tempting as that was, I decided not to do it for three reasons: 1) As much as I'd love to watch him crash and burn, it would be even more fun to see him go crazy wondering when it was going to happen. 2) I owned 20 percent of that game stream, and with Cam's luck, he was going to end up a trillionaire. And 3) As much as I wanted him to suffer, I didn't want him to suffer *too* much. He was my brother, after all. I just wanted him to remember that if I took him on, he would lose and lose huge.

I was even better than him at video games. That was something he knew well and chose to ignore. It drove him nuts that I gave up what he was basing his entire life on. He just couldn't understand it.

Even though I wasn't a gamer anymore, I started

following GameFox229 on my iPad. It wasn't hard to predict when he was going online. Every time Mom and Dad were at work and my brother and one or two of his Awful Threesome mates smuggled that beaver into the basement, you could be pretty sure that GameFox229 was about to hit the World Wide Web.

I'd been there when Cam took his stream online, but nothing could have prepared me for how the GameFox setup really looked to someone watching on the Internet. Cam appeared in such a small box that it almost looked like he was locked in a tiny closet. Elvis wriggled all over him, rubbing up against him and slapping him with his tail. It was chaotic, yet it seemed like it was choreographed, a weird ritual dance. Maybe that was because their eyes moved totally in unison, since they were both watching the same thing—the game action on the screen. It wasn't good exactly, but it was guaranteed to be unique. A gummy-worm-slurping superhero with a rodent sidekick? Please.

About the game action: It was definitely *Guardians*, but it was *different*. Cam was right about that, not that it took a genius to notice the changes. His online followers seemed to be fixated on that. They couldn't wait to see GameFox229 reach Level 13. Our old *Guardians* only went up to 12, so the whole thing was news to me. But Cam's audience believed that he had some rare version—maybe the only one in existence—and Level 13 would reveal the meaning of life or something. Ha ha. Gamers weren't that deep.

It sounded far-fetched to me. Still, one thing about it rang perfectly true: Only my brother could be lucky enough to buy a cast-off old game from the library's throw-away table and wind up with a priceless one-of-a-kind collectible. Jealous? You bet I was. When I bought junk, junk was what I got. When he bought junk, he got treasure, because he was born with a horseshoe up his diaper.

Sigh.

Anyway, real or not, Level 13 was the main reason why GameFox229 was attracting so many followers. The numbers were climbing at an amazing rate. When I checked in on Tuesday, he had about 3,500. By Thursday, it was almost 6,000. When I tried to log out, a pop-up appeared, encouraging me to upgrade my status from "follower" to "subscriber" for only five dollars a month. It promised that only full subscribers would have "premium access" to ask Cam questions at the magical moment he reached Level 13.

Who knew how long he could draw that out? If he got there too fast, he could end his run before attracting the maximum audience. But if progress was too slow, his followers might lose interest and drop off. Or there was another possibility: When I walked in on him the other night, he was playing at a higher level, but he was having a tough time. Maybe the reason he hadn't reached 13 yet was because he *couldn't*.

I exed out of the website in disgust. No way was I going to let my crook of a brother shake me down for five bucks a month for something I could see for free in Technicolor and Smell-O-Vision just by walking down the basement stairs.

On the other hand, I had a 20 percent cut of GameFox229, so a dollar of every one of those five should be coming to me. The whole thing seemed so artificial that it was hard to believe Cam was going to see one cent out of it. But this was Cam. The P.A.G. started out artificial, too, and now it had 874 members. When he got mixed up in things—even dumb things—they could balloon to *Hindenburg* size in the blink of an eye.

Then again, remember what happened to the *Hindenburg*.

CHAPTER SIXTEEN
PAVEL DYSAN

The Awesome Threesome was falling apart.

Technically, that was more than just my opinion. It was a cold, hard fact. The friendship that had grown with us from preschool to elementary school to middle school was on the rocks.

It would be too easy to blame the whole thing on Chuck, even though it was mostly his fault. Well, not Chuck; Duckne. He was Daphne's animal now. Every time she crooked her little finger, he went running. Friends didn't mean anything to him anymore.

Cam once called the boyfriend thing a disease. He was just complaining, but it made more sense to me every day. I kept seeing it as it might appear in a medical textbook or on WebMD:

BOYFRIENDITIS: A debilitating syndrome primarily affecting adolescent boys with very little brainpower. See also: Kinsey, Chuck.

SYMPTOMS: The boyfrienditis patient allows himself to be led around by the nose, usually by a sufferer of a related illness, girlfrienditis. In the most severe cases, the patient forgets his loyalty to his friends, not to mention his hobbies, interests, and everything that ever meant anything to him B.G. (Before Girlfriend). It is the total end of his life as he knows it.

If that sounded a little bitter, then too bad. Chuck had earned it—or at least *Chucky* had. The sad part was, I'd given up arguing with him. It was like chewing out a guy with a broken leg because he couldn't dance. We probably wouldn't have had anything to do with each other at all if it weren't for GameFox229. We were both helping Cam— that was our last connection. And Duckne was leeching into that, too.

It went without saying that Daphne would freak out if she ever learned that Cam was using Elvis for his stream. Fine—that was just reason one of five hundred for not telling her anything about it. But now it was *Chuck* whining about Elvis's welfare and the exploitation of animals. It was almost like he'd been Daphne's boyfriend for so long that he was turning into Daphne! I could only imagine how *that* would look on WebMD:

WARNING: In extreme cases of boyfriend-itis, the sufferer actually takes on the traits and characteristics of his girlfriend. See also: idiot, blithering.

I wanted to say, "What are you going to do? Kidnap the beaver and hide him in your closet?" (Judging by the smell in Cam's basement during streaming sessions, Mrs. Kinsey would really love that.) But I was done arguing with Chuck—and I didn't want to give him any ideas, either. I barely knew the guy these days. He might be crazy enough to attempt a rescue.

Tempting as it was to blame Duckne, the more I thought about it, the more it seemed like Cam was the real problem. He wasn't doing anything wrong; it was more like he'd stopped doing *right*. The Awesome Threesome was more than gummy worms and video games, but Cam's *attitude* toward video games—his famous lifestyle—had always been the glue that held us together. We shared the games, sure—whether we were playing console games, computer games, apps on our phones, or even the little-kid stuff we loved when we were younger. But what we really shared was the *identity* the games gave us. It was who we were.

GameFox229 changed all that. *We* weren't streaming. It was just Cam. And while, technically, it amounted to more time in front of a console than ever before, it wasn't fun anymore. Was the mask on straight? Were the newspapers in place under the couch? Was the webcam aimed properly? How strong was the Wi-Fi signal? Were our phones silenced? Did Cam's cheeks need fresh gummy worms? Which of the hundreds of live messages should he respond to? Were enough people watching? How could we convince more followers to subscribe?

By the time GameFox229 logged out, my neck and shoulders ached from the sheer tension of keeping up with everything. When Cam pulled off his mask, his face glistened with sweat, and his eyes were red from concentrating on the screen. His hands were tensed, his fingers still poking at an imaginary controller. We were exhausted, but he couldn't rest because it took both of us to control Elvis. Lately, the beaver had been getting really upset whenever the gaming finished and the monitor went dark. For sure, we got no help from Chucky, who was already on his phone answering texts from Daphne. He had a lot of explaining to do, since she had probably visited the habitat in the last couple of hours, and found Elvis missing again. Chuck was stressed, thumbs flying, texting excuses that were 90 percent lies. *I* was stressed, wrestling an angry beaver with my aching muscles. And Cam was the most stressed of all.

He spat out two half-chewed gummy worms onto the newspapers on the floor. "Yecch! Gross!"

That did it for me. The person who gave me my first gummy worm now thought they were gross?

"Look at yourself," I panted, cramming an outraged Elvis into the carrier. "Is this the lifestyle you're always going on and on about? What's so great about this that you have to beat your brains out to protect it?"

"Are you bugging?" he crowed. "Didn't you see those numbers? There were more than ten thousand people watching us today!"

"You mean watching *you*," I retorted. "And not even you—some kid in a mask with his trusty rodent by his side. If they could see the real you, they'd send an ambulance. Your eyes are crazy bloodshot and sinking back into your skull. If you were playing zombies, you'd fit right in."

"Hey, how do you spell *hygienist*?" Chuck interjected. "I'm telling Daphne I'm at the dentist."

"You said that last week," I reminded him.

"Oh—right!" Backspacing madly. "How many *k*'s in *chiropractor*?"

I tuned him out and wheeled on Cam. "You know the story about the guy who can't see the forest for the trees? Well, I think you're so obsessed with your lifestyle that you can't see that this isn't it."

Cam was outraged. "You of all people should know that I'm doing exactly what I've always wanted to do! I've got fifteen thousand total followers; over a thousand full subscribers. It's—awesome." As he said that, a yawn twisted his mouth. "Why can't you be happy for me?"

How could I ever explain it to him? The biggest knock on Cam had always been that he was a slacker. I never disagreed with that. He wasn't just a slacker; he was *the* slacker. For Cam, slacking was a symphony, and he was Mozart.

But since GameFox229, the guy was streaming two hours every day after school, and upward of four on the weekends. Add in the setup and strike-down time, plus beaver transport, and Cam was working every free second of his life.

Working—that was the key word. Video games used to be fun. Now they were a full-time job. And anyone who worked as much or as hard as Cam wasn't a slacker anymore.

What chance did the Awesome Threesome have without our slacker-in-chief?

CHAPTER SEVENTEEN
CAMERON BOXER

The numbers were actually insane.

By Sunday, GameFox229 had passed 30,000 followers. Even more important, thousands of them were *subscribing*. I was making real money. Well, I would be when the gaming network paid me my cut, which happened every three months. Royalties, they called it—like I was a prince or something. A kid wasn't supposed to "monetize" an account without adult approval, but luckily, Mr. Fanwhatnot took care of that for me. To be honest, he didn't know it had anything to do with streaming; he thought he was authorizing the P.A.G. to accept online donations for the library.

So I was pretty proud of the work I'd put in to make this happen. When the first check arrived, I wasn't going to cash it; I planned to frame it and put it up on my wall.

Melody put the kibosh on that idea. "Only eighty percent of that money is yours," she reminded me. "You do what you please with your share, but I expect mine in cold, hard cash."

"Be reasonable," I pleaded. "They don't let you cash just twenty percent of a check."

"That's your problem," she informed me. "You shouldn't have made the deal if you weren't willing to live by it."

I already knew that my sister was a gangster, but it was upsetting to see how greedy she was. I wasn't in this for the money, except that enough money would mean I could continue my lifestyle without any of the annoying stuff like getting a job. But Melody just wanted money so she could dump it in a bathtub and swim in it, or whatever the super-rich did.

I was happy—but not totally. Deep down, I knew most of my audience was only watching for a chance to see Level 13. And I was nervous, too, because I was starting to wonder if I was ever going to make it past Level 12. True gamers loved the hardest games because they tested our abilities to the max. Beating a really tough game was like climbing a mountain—you could stand on the top and look down at all the obstacles you had to overcome to get there. But the original *Guardians* was *so* hard it was like a mountain that didn't even have a top. Every time you got close, they'd just add extra mountain.

This wasn't an easy thing to admit. There had never been a game that I couldn't get the hang of sooner or later. And remember—it wasn't just me. The great Draja Dubrovnik never made it to Level 13. I could understand why. You'd slog through lava swamps, fighting off swarms of hornets with lasers and nuclear-armed aphids. And just when the Hive Dome was looking a little closer, a *Bombyx mori* caterpillar would wrap you up in antimatter silk, and by the time you cut your way out of it, you were back at Level 9. I tried again and again. Every time I made it a little farther, some new kind of Geldorfian would come and wreck me. Google says there are as many as 30 million species of insects out there. So the game designers would never run out of different kinds of aliens to throw at me. I was starting to believe that this game was actually impossible, and the people who said they'd made it to Level 13 were lying. Or was I just thinking that to make myself feel better because I was failing so miserably?

Even Elvis was getting frustrated. The beaver seemed to have a sixth sense for when a game wasn't going well. Sometimes, he would jump down from the couch and scurry right up to the TV like he was searching for a solution. At this point, I would have gratefully accepted advice from anybody—beavers included—if I thought it would help. But when Elvis abandoned the couch like that, he also took himself out of the camera shot, and pretty soon there would be complaints in the comment feed.

The future looked grim. When my followers realized that I was never going to reach Level 13, they were going to drop GameFox229 like a bad habit. Bye-bye, royalties, even if all I got was 80 percent. It would be back to the days when my total audience was Pavel, Chuck, and my phone. And I wasn't even so sure about Chuck these days, what with all his lectures on animal exploitation. Like he was Elvis's lawyer or something.

Level 13 was starting to seep into my life even when I wasn't playing *Guardians*. I couldn't sleep at night because my head was whirling with earwigs and mayflies and praying mantises until my skin crawled. I lay awake, beating my brains out over what I was doing wrong. Was there some weapon I wasn't using? Some strategy I was overlooking? Some way to zig instead of zag? I woke up in the morning with bags under my eyes. If this went on, they were going to turn into suitcases. The dull headache behind my eyes was becoming permanent. It felt almost like the flu, with chills, sore muscles, and even nausea—although that might have been the sickening-sweet aftertaste of gummy worms in my stomach. How did I ever love that stuff? I must have been out of my mind!

My energy level was way down, but I didn't let it affect my streaming. I had to be lively and funny and yakking a mile a minute to keep my audience happy. Try that on three hours' sleep with a pounding head and a beaver pummeling you with his tail because he thinks he knows the game better than you do.

And through it all, the comments poured down my computer screen:

I can't believe we're actually going to see it . . .
Level 13, can't wait!
Come on, man, don't keep us in suspense.
Lucky 13, here we come . . .

Did my followers realize they were pushing me toward content that was once considered so unwatchable that forty-seven state governments had to outlaw the game? It was impossible to know. Pavel really had to dig to learn the story of how Level 13 had been banned in the first place. But he hadn't been able to find one word explaining what was so terrible that no one was allowed to play it.

The whole situation was stressful to the point that I actually started *liking* school. Seriously, it was the one place where nothing was expected of me. I had off-loaded my P.A.G. responsibilities onto Daphne, and all those other paggers were giving me plenty of space because they knew I was struggling to bring up my grades. And the work was no problem. Every day, finished assignments appeared in my email inbox. All I had to do was put my own name on them and hand them in electronically to my various teachers.

Sometimes I'd get more than one version of the same worksheet or essay. Then I'd have to read them over and choose the best one. Occasionally, I had to flip a coin. I felt a little bad for the paggers who did all that work for nothing. I wished there was a way to get everybody organized so there would be no duplicate projects and nobody's time would get wasted. But when I tried to bring up the subject with a couple of people, I got the impression that my helpers didn't really know about each other. Plenty of kids were doing it, but they all seemed to think they were the only ones.

It occurred to me: If word got around that so many paggers were giving me free work, they might stop. Worse, they might get mad—which would be really unfair, because I'd never asked them to help in the first place. They just did it on their own—maybe because the P.A.G. had taught them so much about helping. Whatever the reason, I decided that the best thing was to keep my mouth shut and not mess with a system that was chugging along really well. Pretty soon, things would calm down with GameFox229, and I could go back to doing my own homework. If only I could figure out how to beat Level 12 and get to 13!

Another reason I was appreciating school: In my sleep-deprived state, it turned out to be a great place to catch a little catnap now and then. Teachers didn't like it when you dozed off in class, but if you could keep from snoring, you could manage to close your eyes for a couple of minutes and seem like you were just thinking really hard. Plus, on Friday mornings we had an assembly where Dr. LaPierre would stand at the podium and drone on forever. That was totally restful.

This one time I must have fallen asleep in Spanish, because when I woke up, the room was empty except for whoever was gently shaking my shoulder.

"No hablo ingles," I murmured.

"Late night last night, Cameron?" chuckled an adult's voice.

That woke me up in hurry. It was Mr. Fan-doodle! I scrambled up out of my seat and stood facing him. "Hi, Mr. Fan—uh, sir."

"I think I know why you're so tired," he told me. "Come to my office and let's talk about it."

Uh-oh. I hated dealing with the P.A.G.'s faculty adviser for any reason, but this was not good. If Mr. Fan-whatsit knew what all those paggers were doing for me, the end of the world would be right here, right now. I'd spent so much time stressing about the kids clueing in that I never gave a thought to the possibility of a *teacher* figuring it out.

I actually toyed with the idea of running away, although I don't know where I thought I could go. Maybe Elvis would take me in at his habitat. Fat chance—when he realized I hadn't brought the game console, he'd probably throw me out.

Anyway, I followed the guidance counselor into his office and sat down opposite his desk, ready to be sliced and diced.

He said, "Congratulations, Cameron."

Well, that threw me. Was he being sarcastic? Did that mean: *Congratulations, Cameron. In all my years in the school business, you are the worst kid ever!*

"It goes without saying that your teachers are amazed," he went on. "But it wasn't until I'd spoken to every one of them that I was able to understand the full extent of what was happening."

Here it comes, I thought. I was going to fail out of school even worse than I'd told everybody. My parents were going to kill me. GameFox229 was over, and my followers would never get to see Level 13. The only good part was that I wouldn't have to pay Melody 20 percent of the profits, because there wouldn't be any. Too bad I couldn't make her take 20 percent of the blame.

"I'll be honest, Cameron," Mr. Fan-dingus went on. "At first I thought it couldn't be true. But the numbers were right there in front of me. Sure, I've seen students buckle down and pull up their grades before. But never to such a dramatic extent. And certainly not in every subject at the same time."

Huh? My heart, which had been preparing to shut down, resumed its normal rhythm. The beat sounded like: *Not-caught . . . not-caught . . . not-caught.*

So I wasn't found out. Instead, the very opposite had happened. All those paggers were doing such a good job on my homework that the school thought I was a genius! Okay, I'd noticed that the grades coming in on my assignments were a lot better than my usual level. But I was really busy and distracted. And, let's face it, not caring was probably also a factor. Never once did it occur to me that those A's and A-pluses were starting to pile up. Even my test grades were pretty high because I was using notes given to me by some of the smartest kids in the whole school.

The guidance counselor studied me with concerned eyes. "I hope you're more excited about this than you look, because it's really impressive. We've always recognized you as a brilliant student leader. It's good to see you become a brilliant student as well."

"Thanks." I couldn't resist adding, "But don't get mad if it doesn't stay like this forever." For instance, when I started doing my own work again and my A average dropped back to my normal non-genius self.

He smiled. "Modest, as usual. That's another thing we admire about you. But seriously, Cameron, get some sleep. You've got dark circles under your eyes. Don't tell anyone I said this, but good grades aren't everything."

In my case, good grades weren't *anything*. But he was right about the sleep thing. My head was pounding.

The counselor stood up. "Good talk. I won't keep you any longer. I guess I'll see you after school."

I was mystified. "You get a detention for good grades?"

He stared at me for a second and then burst out laughing. "Cameron, you're a riot. The car wash, of course. You're coming, right?"

The car wash. The only problem with Daphne taking over my P.A.G. gig: That girl was an endless source of ideas on how to waste my time. And raise money for the library, obviously.

I could handle the annoying part, but this would keep me away from GameFox229.

I said, "Chances are we'll bump into each other."

Translation: Not in a million years.

I was careful to pack my bag before last period, and to choose a seat at the back of the classroom so I could make my getaway the instant the bell rang. But I chose the wrong exit—a rookie mistake for a pro like me. If I'd been thinking straight, I'd have snuck out at lunch and hidden my bike in the bushes on the opposite side of the school. Then I'd be gone and pedaling furiously for the beaver habitat by now.

But I went out through the parking lot, where the bicycle rack was. There, I found all the teachers' cars moved to the road, replaced by trash cans filled with soapy water. A bucket brigade of kids in bathing suits and T-shirts was already working on the first few vehicles, soaping them up with sponges and mops, rinsing them with hoses, and polishing them with rags and squeegees. Out in the street were even more paggers, flagging down customers and directing them along the driveway into the wash line.

I spun on my heel and tried to sneak back into the building. My reaction time was slower than it used to be— probably a combination of lack of sleep and Level 13. It had made my thinking fuzzier, too. I was usually sharper than this, especially about something that could affect my lifestyle.

"Cam!" came a voice. Daphne was marching toward me like an angry drill sergeant, Chuck on her six, jogging to keep pace. "Where are you going?"

I turned beseeching eyes on Chuck. He knew exactly where I was going—the beaver lodge, followed by my basement. He shot me a helpless expression. When Daphne was up to full speed, he was as useful as a sandbox in the Sahara.

The first excuse to pop into my fevered head was *I'm allergic to soap*. But Daphne was too sharp for that. "I can't get wet!" I blurted. "I think I might be coming down with something, and the temperature is only in the sixties."

It didn't throw Daphne. "Follow me," she said immediately. "I have the perfect job for you."

She and Chuck led me to a line of tables along the brick wall of the school building. A few customers were buying lemonade and snacks while they waited for their cars to be done. At the end of the line sat a student desk with a giant jar of multicolored marbles. A hand-lettered sign declared: HOW MANY MARBLES ARE IN THE JAR? GUESSES $1. WIN A GREAT PRIZE!

"This is you," Daphne informed me.

I turned to Chuck. If he was a true friend, he would get me out of it.

He said, "Nice and dry over here."

I took my seat behind the marbles. People shoved dollars at me, and I wrote down their guesses in a notebook. One lady actually tried to bribe me into giving her the real total, and she didn't believe me when I told her I didn't know. Man, not only didn't I know, but the amount I cared was in the negative numbers. I was missing *streaming* for this! My followers were wondering where I was. Some of them might even have been ready to subscribe today. And where was I? Babysitting a bucket of marbles.

To make matters worse, as soon as all those paggers saw me at the table, they started coming over. It was the library fund-raiser all over again—how great was I to be volunteering some of my precious study time to support the P.A.G.

"You are, legit, an inspiration," String told me. "You've got the crummiest job in the whole car wash, and you're doing it with style!" He stood there, regarding me expectantly.

So I told him exactly what he wanted to hear. "Nobody polishes chrome like The String."

And he went off happy.

My eyelids drooped. Bad enough I was missing out on GameFox229, but I was also having trouble staying awake.

A visit from Xavier woke me up a little. "How'd you do on the science quiz yesterday?"

"A-minus," I told him cautiously.

He beamed with pride, because he'd sent me his study notes. And I had studied—just not from Xavier's notes. Barry Warshovsky was also in that class, and he was even better at science than Xavier.

Pavel was also hanging around, in between his shifts as a windshield squeegee specialist. He was determined to use geometry to figure out the exact number of marbles in the jar.

"So the volume of a cylinder is pi-r-squared times height," he mused. "Of course, the jar isn't a perfect cylinder, and we have to allow for the spaces between the marbles . . ."

"If you say 'pi' one more time, you're getting one in the face," I mumbled. "Like, a custard one."

Through all this, my head was pounding, exhaustion creeping up on me as Pavel murmured calculations in my ear. It wasn't the most relaxing place in town, with soaked and sudsy paggers yelling instructions to each other, and car engines starting up, and waiting customers chit-chatting all over the place, but I suddenly found myself plastered to the chair in a state so drowsy that I might as well have been in a coma.

That was when I saw him. He was probably in his thirties, tall and rail thin, with dark hair, dark eyes, and a black mustache and goatee accentuating pale, pale skin. He was standing in a group of customers, sipping a paper cup of lemonade, and he was staring directly at me. *Only* me—his searing gaze burning holes in my skin.

The next thing I knew, Pavel was shaking my shoulder. "Cam, wake up! I've got it—856 marbles."

I sat bolt upright, blinking in the bright sun. "That guy! Where's the guy?"

"What guy?"

I looked around in dismay, peering into all the adult faces. He was nowhere to be seen—the ghostlike man with the laser eyes.

"Didn't you see him?" I demanded. "Tall guy, super skinny. Jet-black beard, paper-white skin?"

Pavel shook his head. "There's nobody here like that. Maybe you just dreamed it."

"Yeah, maybe."

Mr. Fan-widget was right. I needed to get more sleep.

CHAPTER EIGHTEEN
MELODY BOXER

On Monday afternoon. I went over to my friend Katrina's to work on our social studies project. I had to ring the bell five times before she finally showed up to let me in.

"Sorry," she said airily. "There's this guy on the Internet. You've got to see it!"

As I followed her up the stairs to her room, she filled me in on the details: "It's a game stream, but the guy has a pet beaver—remember when the P.A.G. built that habitat for Elvis? Kind of like him. Only he watches the guy gaming and gets totally into it . . ."

And I just knew. Oh, sure, I allowed myself to believe—hope, mostly—that this would turn out to be some other wing nut with a beaver. But no, it was Cam. Who else? If my brother started a stream, it was only a matter of time before the whole world was watching him.

Actually, I was kind of surprised Katrina didn't recognize Cam. He was wearing a Zorro mask, not a moose head. She *knew* my brother. And it was his voice, even if it was garbled by a mouthful of gummy worms. But I guess you didn't see what you weren't expecting to. Either that, or Cam was better at disguises than I gave him credit for.

Sigh.

Katrina let out a peal of laughter as Cam's character traded rocket fire with a seven-foot praying mantis, and in the corner box, Elvis jumped up and down like an excited toddler. "Isn't it amazing?" she enthused.

"I'm amazed," I agreed. It was the truth. My eyes found the counter at the top, and I nearly swallowed my tongue. Katrina and I weren't the only idiots staring at Cam and Elvis. At this moment, 43,271 computers and mobile devices around the world were tuned in to the stream. I actually blinked and checked it again to make sure I wasn't seeing things. Now the counter said 43,283. In the time it took me to come to terms with the fact that my brother was getting famous, a dozen more people had signed on. And that wasn't even his entire following; it was just the people watching right now!

"It's called GameFox229," Katrina explained. "I think that must be the guy. Fox is a pretty dumb name for a beaver."

"It's all pretty dumb to me," I mumbled. Or maybe it wasn't so dumb. Had anyone ever lived such a charmed life as Cameron Boxer?

Of course, I was supposed to get 20 percent of everything he earned. Why was I so consumed with rage? Maybe because he was so lucky that something was bound to come up that meant he wouldn't have to pay me. Or maybe the money had nothing to do with it, and I was just mad because my brother was getting exactly what he wanted. Again.

We accomplished next to nothing. I was too furious to concentrate, and Katrina insisted on following Cam's stream, muted, while we worked. Even with the volume off, it was unbearable. I couldn't get past the fact that if there had been sound, it would be *him*. It took all my restraint not to pick up Katrina's field hockey stick and heave it like a javelin through her computer screen.

Mr. Bundy came back with a pizza, but I turned down their offer to stay, and started for home. For some reason, it felt very important to yell at Cam. I had no idea what I planned to say to him, except whatever it was, it was going to be loud.

I was so focused on planning my tirade that I almost missed Cam when he flashed by on his bike, Elvis's carrier in the basket.

I wheeled around and barked, *"Cam!"*

I must have startled him, because he went into a spectacular wipeout. But—that luck again—he ended up in the soft earth of a flower bed. The carrier bounced a couple of times, but it was okay. Elvis was shaken but unhurt.

"Where's your limo?" I snarled. "GameFox229 is way too rich and famous for pedal power."

"Shhh!" he hissed. "Somebody will hear you!"

"Oh, too bad," I retorted sarcastically. "If you're trying to keep a secret, maybe you shouldn't go on the Internet in front of *forty-three thousand people!*"

He dragged himself out of the flowers, rescued Elvis, and picked up his bike. "What are you freaking out about? You know I stream."

"Yeah, but you didn't tell me you were some kind of rock star at it!"

He just shrugged, mystified, and for an instant, I saw that I was the one acting crazy, not him. After all, what difference should it make to me if he streamed for forty followers or forty thousand?

I calmed down a little. "Seriously, Cam, I just came from Katrina's. Guess what? She's a GameFox fan."

He blanched. "You didn't tell her?"

I shook my head. "She found the stream on her own. She doesn't know it's you, and I'm not going to blab. But you've got to figure if Katrina stumbled on GameFox229, other kids from town will, too. And not all of them will think it's a coincidence you've got a beaver just like Elvis."

He nodded gravely, and I got a clear view of his face in the late afternoon shadows. Sure, Cam and I lived under the same roof. But we'd been doing that for so long that I guess I never really looked at him. He seemed thinner and older, with dark circles under his eyes. Weary. Unhappy. *Unhealthy.*

"Have you seen yourself in a mirror lately?" I asked.

"What's that supposed to mean?"

"Are you sick?" I persisted. "You're skinny, you never smile, your face is the color of Cream of Wheat. I've seen extras on *The Walking Dead* who are in better shape than you."

He brushed some more dirt off his jeans. "I fell off my bike—thanks to *you*."

"That's part of it," I reasoned. "How come you're wound up so tight that all I had to do was call your name to send you flying into the ditch? However famous you're getting as a streamer—if this is what it's doing to you, it isn't worth it!"

"So that's what this is really about," he told me. "You can't stand it because the stream is taking off. Well, don't worry—you'll get your twenty percent!"

"I don't want my twenty percent," I retorted. "I want my brother back!"

"Yeah—that's a laugh." He settled Elvis's carrier in the basket, climbed back on the bike, and rode off in the direction of the habitat.

As I watched him go, I realized that I wasn't quite so jealous of Cam anymore.

I was worried about him.

CHAPTER NINETEEN
CHUCK KINSEY

It wasn't good . . . and it was only going to get worse.

Elvis still wasn't gaining back any of his winter weight, and Daphne was coming unglued over it. She was convinced that the beaver's long hours away from the habitat meant that he was out there looking for a mate, and she couldn't understand why he hadn't found one yet.

"Maybe there aren't any other single beavers around here." Sure, I knew how lame that sounded. But what was I supposed to tell her? The truth?

"He's depressed," she concluded sadly. "That's why he isn't eating well."

Half of Daphne's attention was on Elvis, and the other half was concerned with running the P.A.G. So there was nothing left for our relationship.

That didn't make me very happy—especially because I couldn't focus on the Awesome Threesome, either. Pavel and I weren't getting along. And Cam was kind of lost to both of us. Not that we didn't see him—we helped out with GameFox229 whenever we could. But the stream was going gangbusters, and instead of being happy about it, Cam just seemed to get more tense and nervous.

These days, it was nothing for him and Elvis to have an audience of 100,000 or more. There were 20,000 full, paying subscribers. It wasn't a dream anymore or even a hobby. It was a business, and Cam was totally swept away in it.

I got a reality check on that during my free period on Thursday. I was on the way to the cafeteria to buy a granola bar—Daphne said I needed more fiber in my diet. As I cut through the seventh-grade Hallway of Heroes, I noticed a new picture up by the ceiling, over the fire extinguisher.

They were mostly celebrities—actors, athletes, YouTubers, politicians. Singers, rappers, an opera star. There were historical figures, too—Alexander Hamilton, Shakespeare, Nelson Mandela. There were a few photographs of students' moms and dads who were overseas with the military. And—

At first, I almost walked right past it. It was a screenshot of GameFox229. Not the greatest photograph in the world—grainy and pixelated, the product of a cheap printer. But there was no mistaking the subject matter—Cam in the Zorro mask, his cheeks puffed out with gummy worms, Elvis peering down from his shoulder.

This was bad—and in so many ways. First, it meant that Cam's stream was getting so famous that his fans were everywhere—even random kids in a random town like ours. Cam always wanted a lot of followers, but I didn't think it had ever occurred to him that some of those followers could turn out to be the same people he needed to hide his streaming from. Second, if I could see Cam plain as day behind that mask, how long would it take before somebody else connected the dots? Finally, Cam was disguised, but Elvis wasn't. Okay, all beavers look alike, but kids in Sycamore didn't know all beavers. They only knew one—the one whose habitat they'd helped to build.

I set my jaw. That picture had to come down before Daphne saw it. She might not be able to recognize Cam, but she had memorized every hair on Elvis's head. One look at the beaver was all it would take for her to make a positive identification. Then, once she started filling in the blanks, there'd be no stopping her: Elvis to Cam, and on to me—her lying boyfriend, who was actively helping in the ruse.

I leaped at the wall, but my reaching fingers fell a few inches short of the high picture. I didn't give up. I wasn't just fighting for Cam's lifestyle; I was fighting for my own. Duckne was at stake here. My ship was sinking.

I ran into an empty classroom and came back with a wooden chair. I jumped up on it, pulled down the GameFox229 picture, and tore it into a million pieces on the spot. I was determined that not one single shred of it would be large enough to be noticed by microscope, much less recognized as Elvis or Cam. I tore until my fingers were sore and there was nothing left but a scatter of confetti on the floor.

I was so focused on doing the job and doing it right that the voice startled me. "Chuck, what's going on?"

I whipped around so fast that I fell off the chair and landed in a cloud of GameFox229 dust. There stood Mr. Fanshaw, watching me disapprovingly.

"Did you deliberately destroy somebody's picture?" he demanded.

If I was smart like Pavel, I probably could have come up with a really good explanation for why I was there and what I was doing. But all I could think of was, "I don't know."

"The Hallway of Heroes is a place where students can express what's important to them. Why would you spoil that?"

I had an explanation, but I couldn't very well give it: That however important it was to some kid to put GameFox229 on the wall, it was ten times more important to me that Daphne should never see it. So I doubled down on my original answer: "I don't know."

From there, I just stuck with it. What was it about the picture that upset me so much? "I don't know." How could I show such disrespect to the person who put it there? "I don't know."

Mr. Fanshaw was one of those adults who never lost his temper, but this time he really wanted to. I could tell. His face kept getting redder as he asked me over and over again what the picture was and why I hated it enough to tear it up.

"I don't know," I replied.

He finally surrendered, but not before giving me a week of detention and an order to replace that picture ASAP. I cut a full-page photograph out of *Rolling Stone* magazine and stuck it up there. I thought it was a rock star, but it turned out to be an ad for anti-constipation pills. No wonder the guy was smiling.

Considering I did all this for Daphne, she was pretty ticked off at me. I couldn't tell her what my detentions were really for, so I told her I got into a fight.

She was horrified. "Chucky—you never resort to *violence* to solve a problem! What were you thinking?"

I wasn't proud of it, but I kind of gave her the impression that I was defending her against someone who said she was doing a lousy job running the P.A.G.

I was off the hook after that. And I kind of got a kick out of walking down the hall and seeing the smiling unconstipated guy.

But I still had the detentions to serve, and those weren't fun. Basically, you just sat there with your fellow criminals in this little room, which, for some reason, was twenty degrees hotter than any other part of the school. You could read, or do homework, or count the holes in the ceiling tiles—it was all the same to Mrs. Warden. Yes, that was her name. They picked a Warden to run the after-school jail. If anybody else thought that was weird, they didn't say.

Mrs. Warden ran detention, but she wasn't *in* detention, which meant that she didn't have to stay in the room the whole time. She probably went down to the cafeteria to cool herself off in the freezer. As soon as she left, everybody pulled out their phones except me.

"It's cool, man," String assured me. He was serving time for making an "offensive" sculpture out of athletic tape in the locker room. "She won't be back for a while."

I was determined to resist the temptation. The last thing I needed was to get caught breaking the no-phones rule on the very first day and end up with an even longer sentence in this sweat lodge.

But then my pocket started vibrating. I was getting a call. I produced the phone and turned my back to the door to cover myself in case the Warden showed up.

It was Cam, FaceTiming from the bike rack in the parking lot. "Where are you, man? It's time to get Elvis."

"I'm in the detention room," I whispered.

He sounded irritated. "What are you doing there?"

"I'm panning for gold. What do you think I'm doing?" I explained how Mr. Fanshaw had caught me tearing down the GameFox229 picture from the Hallway of Heroes.

"GameFox?" String overheard the name. "Yo, man— you watch that, too? That guy's *fire!*"

"Yeah, fire," I agreed lamely, wishing I'd been quieter.

Cam's tone totally changed. "You did the right thing, Chuck. If a bigmouth like Daphne ever saw it—"

"That's my girlfriend you're talking about!" I interrupted.

"Okay, okay. I can get Elvis myself. But come by the house as soon as you can. I'm going to need your help with the message scroll while I'm streaming." We'd done our time. Luckily, I had my bike at school for Elvis so I was able to get to Cam's place in a matter of minutes.

The basement was bedlam. Cam was battling aliens at a frantic pace, and talking a mile a minute around the gummy worms in his cheeks. Elvis was more animated than I'd ever seen him, his front paws working furiously, as if in hand-to-hand combat with the Geldorfian warrior moths on the screen. Cam nearly blew his stack when Elvis suddenly tail-slapped the game controller out of his hands. But a few seconds later, one of the comments mentioned that Cam's laser was set on the wrong frequency. Cam would have blown up his own ship if he'd fired it.

The feed lit up: *The beaver is a genius! . . . Great move, buddy! . . . That's using what nature gave you!*

Daphne always said Elvis was smart. She didn't know the half of it.

I grabbed a marker and began scribbling down questions for Cam to respond to. I doubt I was able to manage one in twenty. The comments were scrolling so fast that I could barely keep up. A glance at the counter explained why. More than 140,000 people were following the stream this afternoon, the biggest audience ever. Pavel should see this! But of course, Pavel would probably be assisting Cam next time, when the audience was likely to be even bigger. I felt a twinge of regret at the thought of my almost-but-not-quite ex-friend.

When it was over, we biked Elvis back to the woods. The beaver pounded the water with his tail, spraying us. He'd been getting upset lately at the end of streaming sessions. Maybe this was his way of teaching us a lesson.

"Elvis?" came a distant voice at the sound of the splashing.

"It's Daphne!" I hissed. "Run!"

Cam took off like a shot for the opening in the trees where we'd left our bikes. I was hot on his heels. An exposed root snagged my foot, and I went down hard, seeing stars. By the time my vision cleared, Cam was nowhere to be seen. I leaped up to continue the escape.

"Chucky?"

I had to think fast, which wasn't something I was good at. So I blurted, "I don't know!" maybe because it had worked on Mr. Fanshaw. Then I realized that Daphne hadn't asked anything yet. I just started babbling. "I—Elvis—woods—"

She threw her arms around me and gave me a big hug. "I understand. You're checking on Elvis for me. That's so sweet."

Luckily, Cam had the pet carrier. *I don't know* wouldn't have worked as an explanation for that.

I left Daphne with Elvis and made my way out of the woods to the spot where we'd parked the bikes. I figured Cam would be long gone, but he was right there, standing stock-still, staring off down the road. His face was chalk white, a mask of horror.

"What's the matter?" I asked in alarm.

"I just saw him," he replied, his voice reedy. "The guy."

"What guy?"

"The one who was staring at me on car-wash day. I didn't dream him. He's out there."

CHAPTER TWENTY
CAMERON BOXER

I knew it! I hadn't hallucinated the guy who'd been staring at me at the P.A.G. car wash. No imagination could invent a creep like that—paper-white skin covering a bony face that was barely more than a skull. Sunken, beady eyes. Jet-black hair and goatee. He was real, right here in Sycamore. And he was after me.

The second time I saw him was when Daphne caught us at the beaver habitat and Chuck sacrificed himself so I could get away. I was climbing onto my bike when I detected a shiny black SUV coming along the road from the direction of the freeway. As soon as the driver spotted me he slowed down until he was barely moving. The power window began to sink into the door, and there he was—the guy, with those scary black eyes fixed on me.

I froze. Even as the SUV inched forward, his eyes never left me.

I started to backpedal into the underbrush, but then I remembered: Daphne was in the woods—in her own way, almost as scary as the guy. So I was stuck there, a sitting duck. If it weren't for that giant lumber truck coming up behind the SUV and honking, who knows what could have happened?

My relief lasted only a few hours. Loading the dishwasher after dinner, I could have sworn I saw the same SUV parked on the street just down the block from our house. Was it *him*? If so, it meant he knew where I lived!

I spent the rest of the evening and half the night up in the attic, peering out the window through Mom's bird-watching binoculars. By then, the SUV was gone . . . but what if the guy had parked it somewhere else because he knew I was onto him? He could have come back on foot.

Dad caught me there just after midnight. "What are you doing, Cam?"

I was so startled that I straightened up suddenly and smashed my head on a low beam. It didn't do my headache any good. I saw stars—and some of them weren't in the sky.

Which gave me an idea. "I'm doing research for my astronomy project."

Dad frowned. "You're not taking astronomy."

"It's science," I amended quickly. "We're doing a unit on the night sky." I regarded him uneasily while my head pounded and the fireworks behind my eyes died down. "How do you know so much about my classes?" Melody and I always assumed that Mom and Dad worked twenty-five hours a day at the store. Since when did they have time to snoop on our schoolwork?

"Your guidance counselor called," he explained. "That Mr. Fanshaw. He wanted to make sure we didn't miss the posting of your progress report. Amazing—I can't believe the grades you're getting!"

For a moment, I thought he was being sarcastic. In my brain-scrambled state, it took a second to remember that I was pulling straight A's.

"I owe you an apology, Cam," Dad went on. "I was convinced that you'd never bring up your grades until you cut back on the gaming. I've got to hand it to you—you're doing both, and you're killing it. But take a word of advice from an old man who works too hard: You're burning the candle at both ends. Mom's noticed it, too. She thinks you've dropped a little weight."

Yeah, me and Elvis, I reflected silently.

"Give yourself a break," Dad advised. "Shave a little off your gaming time, a little off your studying time, and find a happy medium." He ruffled my hair, but then dropped his hand to my forehead. "You're burning up, kid! Are you running a fever?"

"Fever? Me?" I'd never thought about it, but it kind of made sense. All the problems I'd been having—headache, chills, sore muscles, waking up in a cold sweat—those were common fever symptoms.

But I didn't have time for a fever. If Mom got wind of this, I'd be in bed for a week, taking chicken soup through an IV tube. To a mother, the word *fever* was like waving a red cape in front of a bull. You just didn't do it. I could have my head knocked off and Mom wouldn't even notice—not unless she stuck a thermometer in my mouth and it read one hundred plus. Then I'd be on my way to the doctor, the clinic, the emergency room. No way—not with GameFox229 blowing up and the dream of 50,000 subscribers on the verge of becoming reality. If I disappeared now, my audience would think it was because I didn't have what it took to reach Level 13! By the time Mom pronounced me fever-free, my followers would take a nosedive, and my subscribers would melt away to nothing. Nobody wanted to pay cold, hard cash for content they weren't getting.

This had disaster written all over it. I had to get Dad off the scent.

"I'm fine," I told him. "Just a little overheated from going up and down the attic stairs."

"And from lack of sleep," he added. "Hit the sack and we'll see how you are in the morning."

In the morning, I knew, he would be at the store before I even opened my eyes. "Good idea," I told him. "Hey, would you mind not mentioning this to Mom? I don't want to worry her. You know, unless I have to."

"Deal," he said.

I was in the clear, at least for the time being.

That night, I had the weirdest dream. I was sitting at a wooden table across from a dark, shadowy figure. A single bare bulb hung from the ceiling, glaring into my eyes so that I couldn't see anything except the broad-brimmed hat that obscured his face. I asked the figure what it would take for GameFox229 to get to 50,000 subscribers, which seemed like kind of a stupid thing to ask a total stranger.

But he actually had an answer, and it scared me out of my wits. He said in an ice-cold voice that echoed like it was coming out of a tomb: *"The price is your soul."*

I jumped up and my knees overturned the table in front of me. It whacked into the bulb, sending it swinging back and forth on the end of its wire. For a split second, it illuminated my companion's face as it passed. Sunken cheeks, pale skin, black goatee—

The guy!

I came out of the dream like I'd been shot from a cannon. I didn't feel feverish anymore. In fact, the only thing I felt was my heart, which was threatening to pound clear through my rib cage.

Just a dream . . . just a dream . . . I kept telling myself. You couldn't trade your soul in exchange for a successful game stream. But the thought of it was so awful that I could almost see the guy lurking in the dark corners of my room. And every time I closed my eyes, that chilling voice echoed inside my head: *". . . your soul."*

I wanted the light on very badly. But if Dad spotted it in my doorframe, all that fever stuff might come up again. And speaking of fever, I felt worse than ever. My head was throbbing, and I had a stomachache along with it.

No way was I going back to sleep tonight, so I checked my school iPad. Four different kids had sent me the same book report. I tried to read them but I just couldn't—not with my head on fire and my eyes refusing to focus.

I felt like a zombie the whole next day, and when streaming time came after school, I barely had the energy to put on my mask and lift the game controller. If it hadn't been for Pavel, I don't think I could have fought Elvis back into the carrier when it was all over.

"Dude, you look terrible," Pavel told me, his voice strained as he pressed the door shut against the angry beaver's resistance.

"I got maybe three hours' sleep last night." I told him about the dream. "Stupid, I know. But this weird guy around town has really got me freaked out."

I expected him to laugh. Instead, he looked thoughtful.

"What?" I coaxed.

"Uh, nothing, technically," he replied. "But you remember what you said, right? 'I'd do anything—*anything*—to get to 50,000 subscribers.'"

"Well, yeah," I admitted. "But I just meant that 50,000 subscribers would be—you know—really great."

"But that's not what you said," he persisted. "You said you'd do *anything*. Anything means anything. Even— giving up your soul."

I could actually feel myself turning pale—which was a really awful sensation, especially for someone who was pretty pale already. "What are you telling me? That without even knowing it, I traded my soul for subscribers, and this guy is the soul collector, stalking me to pay up?"

"Of course not!" he scoffed. "There's no such thing as a soul collector! Who do you think I am—Chuck?"

I worked up a grin. "He already sold *his* soul—to Duckne."

The subject should have been over, but it hung in the air between us like a bad smell.

I was supposed to feel better now that everything was out in the open. Yet somehow it didn't work out that way.

Pavel was a smart guy, a logical thinker. And sure, he did say there was no such thing as a soul collector. But that was all he said. He didn't have any other explanation of who the mysterious stranger might be.

The worst part was this: I expected Pavel to laugh in my face over the dream and the whole soul thing. He didn't. He took it pretty seriously.

Which told me that I had to take it seriously, too.

CHAPTER TWENTY-ONE
DAPHNE LEIBOWITZ

I was normally an upbeat person, but lately it had been harder and harder to look on the bright side. Maybe it was Elvis who was putting me in a bad mood. He was nothing but fur and bones. I was amazed he had the strength to drag his big flat tail around. You definitely couldn't blame winter weight loss anymore—that was months ago. There was hardly any freshly chewed wood around his habitat, which meant he wasn't doing what he was supposed to be doing. He was still spending long periods of time away from his lodge. But if he was looking for a mate, shouldn't he have found her by now? It was almost as if he had a secret life somewhere else!

It was a good thing I had Chucky. He was a steadying influence. Otherwise, everything would have been negative. Even the Positive Action Group wasn't as positive as it used to be. I had to take a lot of the responsibility for that because I was the acting president. We were supposed to be bringing in money for the new library building, and I had fund-raiser's block. I hadn't had a single new idea since the car wash. Some of the blame for that had to go to Mr. Fanshaw, who wasn't very supportive of my more creative ideas, like selling advertising space on the school buses and renting out spare classrooms through Airbnb. It was depressing to come up with suggestion after suggestion only to be shot down in favor of doing absolutely nothing.

"We're not doing nothing," the guidance counselor insisted. "We're going to school, getting an education, living our lives. The P.A.G. is a wonderful thing, but it can't solve all the world's problems. A new library costs millions, and the budget is almost two hundred thousand dollars short. We're happy to help, but a middle school can't do it all."

And suddenly, I was crying. I couldn't help it. I tried to swallow the tears but they kept coming anyway. "*He'd* find a way!"

"He?" echoed Mr. Fanshaw. "He who?"

"Cam!" I blubbered.

"Cameron Boxer?" He seemed amazed. "Sure, Cameron is a remarkable young man, but he's an eighth grader, just like you. He created the P.A.G., but he didn't give it magic powers. If he were in your shoes right now, he'd be subject to the same limitations."

How could I explain it? I used to think I could be a better student leader than Cam because he missed most of the meetings and never said much when he did show up. More often than not, it seemed like he had no idea what the club was even doing. But he must have, because when Cam was running things, the P.A.G. was *unstoppable*. He came off like a slacker, but he couldn't have been. Just look what we'd accomplished.

Now I was in charge of it, and I was dropping the ball. Not only was I letting down the whole town, but I was also letting down Cam by not getting the job done while he took a break to bring up his grades.

It was a bitter pill to swallow that I wasn't as good as I thought I was. Then again, if you only measured yourself against the kid who founded the P.A.G., you were bound to come off second best.

Besides, I wasn't giving up so easily. I had posters all over the school asking kids for fund-raising suggestions. Obviously, my fellow paggers were just as blocked as their acting president—or maybe the word just wasn't getting out. A few more posters might do the trick. It definitely couldn't hurt.

I headed for the art room. First period was still twenty minutes away. That gave me just enough time to get started on a couple of extra posters. I could place them in spots I hadn't thought of before, but where kids hung out—like the stairwells, the bathrooms, or the parking lot of the 7-Eleven up the block.

The art room was deserted except for big Xavier Meggett, who was hunched over the silk screen. I used to be afraid of Xavier, but working side by side with him showed me what a non-scary person he could be. A lot of kids who didn't fit in found kind of a home in the P.A.G. That went double for Xavier, who'd been held back a couple of years, and had even had problems with the law. Now, not only was he a pagger, but he'd also turned out to be one of the top art students in the whole school.

"Hi, Xavier," I greeted him. "What are you working on?"

"This." He opened the lid of the screener and held up a size 3XL T-shirt. Printed in black ink along the white fabric was the image of a bandit's mask above a single word: *GAMEFOX229.*

"Looks great," I told him. "But what's GameFox229?"

He stared at me. "You don't know? Everybody watches GameFox229. He's the hottest game streamer on the Internet."

"I'm not really into video games," I admitted. "Chucky tried to get me interested a couple of times, but he gave up."

"You don't have to be a gamer to watch GameFox229," Xavier informed me in his low, rumbling voice. "The guy's hilarious. He's got this partner who's a beaver. And get this—the beaver loves video games even more than the human does. So you're watching the game, but you're also watching the beaver watching the game. It's awesome!"

I frowned. "I don't really like the idea of someone using an animal as a trick to get followers on the Internet. It makes me think of Elvis, wasting away at his habitat, poor little guy."

"That's why you'd love it," he insisted. "You like Elvis, right? The beaver reminds me a lot of him. If you've seen one beaver, you've seen them all, I guess."

"Not true," I lectured. "Elvis has a unique personality that comes through if you look at his face . . ." My voice trailed off when I saw that Xavier wasn't really listening. And anyway, he wasn't even talking about Elvis; he was talking about this other beaver on the Internet.

As the day went on, I forgot the whole conversation— the acting president of the P.A.G. had more important things to worry about than a homemade shirt. But later, at lunch, there was a commotion in the cafeteria. Xavier was at the center of a huge crowd. He was wearing the newly designed shirt, which had looked like a bedsheet in the art room, but actually fit him perfectly. Out of the hubbub of voices, one name rose above the others: *GameFox* this, *GameFox* that, "Where'd you get the *GameFox* shirt?" and "How much do you want for it?"

"Not for sale," Xavier announced smugly. "It's one of a kind."

"I'll give you twenty bucks for it," someone called.

"Thirty!"

"Forty!"

"Forget it," said Xavier, obviously thrilled with himself.

"Yeah, back off, losers!" String reached his arm barely halfway around Xavier's massive shoulders. "The not-for-sale thing—that's just for the regular people, right? You'll sell it to The String?"

"Nope," Xavier replied cheerfully and walked off, leaving the lunchroom throng crying out their frustration.

By that time, the plan was fully formed in my mind. How could it not be? I needed a fund-raiser, and here were dozens of kids practically throwing money at Xavier.

I caught up with Xavier in the hall, which wasn't easy, since one of his strides was longer than three of mine. "How many of those T-shirts can you make?" I panted.

"As many as I want," he told me. "I wanted to make one, and I already made it."

"But, Xavier—"

He stopped and faced me. The eyeholes in the mask on his chest seemed to be glaring at me. "I've got a one-of-a-kind shirt. If I make more, it won't be one of a kind anymore."

"It's not for me," I reasoned. "The P.A.G. is in trouble. We haven't had a decent fund-raiser since the car wash. You can change all that—you and your T-shirts."

Well, that made all the difference for Xavier. He was a pagger first, before anything else. The Positive Action Group was back in business—and this time the business would be selling T-shirts with the logo of this streamer everybody seemed to love.

Mr. Fanshaw gave me enough money from the proceeds of the car wash to buy thirty blank tees. But when I asked Chuck to come with me to the store to help carry the shirts, he got all weird about it.

"GameFox229? You know about that?"

"Not really," I admitted. "I just heard about it today. But everybody else does, that's for sure."

"It's a terrible idea," he said quickly. "GameFox229 is lousy. You don't want anything to do with him."

"It's a moneymaker," I explained. "The P.A.G. needs a new fund-raising idea. If that's what sells, I'm all for it."

"No!" he exclaimed urgently. "No one's going to buy these T-shirts. Everybody hates GameFox229. He's the worst streamer on the whole web."

"Are you kidding?" I exploded. "They practically ripped the first one off Xavier's back. One kid offered him forty bucks for it! A skinny little guy—he could have fit his whole family inside Xavier's giant shirt. Here's my plan: The blank tees cost three fifty. We'll sell them for twenty-five dollars. We're going to make a fortune!"

He shut up about it, but I could tell he wasn't happy. Chucky could be really moody sometimes, which was a quality I didn't admire very much in him. I guess that was part of being in a relationship—you had to take the bad with the good.

Our production line was pretty efficient. Xavier silk-screened the new shirts while Chucky and I worked with hand dryers to get them ready for purchase. I figured we could sell them in the cafeteria at lunch.

We never made it that far. Kids were swarming outside the art room, jockeying for position, cash in hand. We unloaded thirty shirts in thirty seconds, most of them not even dry yet. The kids who didn't get one were so angry that Chucky and I would have been torn to pieces if Xavier hadn't been there. Nobody took on Xavier Meggett, not even for a GameFox229 tee.

"Don't worry, you guys," I called to the disappointed crowd. "We'll make more shirts tomorrow."

"No we won't!" Chucky hissed in dismay. "Mr. Fanshaw said thirty shirts, that's it. They're all gone."

"He gave us *money* for thirty shirts," I amended, waving today's take in his face. "Now we have enough cash for every blank tee in town."

He looked like he was going to cry.

"It's for the P.A.G., man," Xavier soothed. "You can't argue with that."

We went shopping again after school, this time with Xavier to help us with the heavy lifting. When the store didn't have any more white tees, we switched to pale colors like yellow, green, blue, and pink. Then it was back into production. The art room ran out of black ink, so Xavier used navy. The next two hundred shirts were gone by lunch, with a hundred more on back order.

When we showed up at the guidance office with three shoeboxes packed with cash, I thought Mr. Fanshaw was going to faint. He looked at us as if he believed we'd robbed a bank.

"There were only thirty shirts," the counselor said weakly. "How much are you charging for them?"

"We took the profits from the first batch and invested in another run," Xavier explained in his deep voice.

Mr. Fanshaw swallowed hard. "But you're done now, right?"

"Actually, we came to ask you for a ride to Walmart," I told him. "There aren't any more blank tees in Sycamore."

"Unless you think—you know—we've done enough," Chucky added.

I could have kicked him for that.

"It's for a good cause," our faculty adviser said faintly. "But that's a lot of cash. Maybe we should stop at the bank on the way to Walmart."

By the end of the week, we'd sold more T-shirts than there were kids in Sycamore Middle School. People were buying them for brothers and sisters, and packing them away to give as gifts. At any given time, two-thirds of the students were wearing the things. Some wore them several days in a row without laundering. On denim day, even some of the teachers sported them with their jeans. The P.A.G. had made over twenty thousand dollars for the library, and my fund-raiser's block was a thing of the past.

It dawned on me that the only person who didn't have a GameFox229 T-shirt was the kid who deserved one more than anybody else—Cam Boxer. If it hadn't been for his shining example, I might never have pushed myself to come up with this great idea.

So we arranged a little ceremony at lunch on Friday to present him with his very own GameFox229 tee while everybody in the cafeteria stood on their chairs and cheered their heads off.

Cam never liked to be the center of attention—he was too modest. This time was no exception. In fact, if it hadn't been for the crowd chanting *"Put it on! Put it ON!"* he would have crammed the shirt into his backpack and ignored the whole thing. When he finally pulled it over his head, the place went wild. Even the lunch ladies came out to join the celebration.

Through it all, Cam looked stunned. It reminded me of Chucky's reaction to this whole T-shirt business. The most successful fund-raiser in the history of the P.A.G., and those two acted as if a crime were being committed.

I'd never understand guys.

CHAPTER TWENTY-TWO
CAMERON BOXER

Ninety-nine-point-eight degrees.

I frowned at the thermometer. Dad was right. I really was feverish these days. Or maybe not—when Melody was a baby, the pediatrician once told Mom that it didn't count unless it was over a hundred. Was that just for toddlers or for all kids, including my age? And did the hundred-degree rule only apply to temperature by butt? In that case, I was never going to find out, that was for sure.

So was I sick or what? I definitely didn't feel great—I still had headaches and muscle aches, and my brain was foggy. But wasn't that just the lack of sleep, the bike rides to and from the beaver habitat, the pressures of GameFox229?

I was starting to question whether this whole streaming thing was worth it. I'd only been at it for a few weeks, and I was already at the end of my rope.

And it didn't help that I wasn't any closer to beating Level 12. The elusive 13 seemed so close that I should have been able to stick my hand into the TV screen and touch it. Instead, it might as well have been in orbit around Geldorf on the opposite side of the galaxy. Reaching it was all I thought about anymore. I wasn't worried about any state laws or "inappropriate content." Sure, I wondered what could possibly be shocking/gross/upsetting/dangerous enough for forty-seven states to ban a harmless video game. But at this point, I was far beyond caring about that—not even if Level 13 contained a killer death ray that vaporized the user.

I used to ache to have something in common with the great Draja Dubrovnik, but not *this*! He never got to Level 13 and it was starting to look like I never would, either. My audience was massive beyond my wildest dreams. I could hit 50,000 subscribers any day now. But as much as my followers loved me, they were growing impatient. An excitable beaver wouldn't distract them forever.

I put away the thermometer and padded back to my room. The GameFox229 T-shirt hung over the back of my desk chair, mocking me. They were all over school. I couldn't walk down a hallway without a half dozen of them coming at me. Yesterday, Dr. LaPierre wore one under his suit jacket.

"Look on the bright side," had been Chuck's advice. "At least it means you've got a lot of fans."

I wasn't interested in Chuck's opinion. I hadn't forgotten his role—and the role of his "shipmate"—in getting Xavier to make those shirts in the first place. If word got around that GameFox229 and I were one and the same, I'd be dead meat. The whole school thought I was sitting alone in my room, cracking book after book after book.

Half the eighth grade was breaking their necks to give me free assignments, not that I'd asked anybody to. But still— I was taking them, wasn't I?

No wonder my head hurt!

I was so wound up that when the doorbell rang, I practically went through the ceiling.

"Get that, will you?" I called to Melody.

"I'm busy!" she shouted back.

"I'm busier than you! Get the door!"

When I heard her on the stairs, I glanced out my window—and froze in shock. There, parked at the curb, was the black SUV. I pressed up against the glass and peered straight down.

It was him—the *stalker*—right on our stoop! I could actually make out his pale skin and black goatee!

"Melody!" I exclaimed in a stage whisper. "Stop!"

Her slippers left the carpeted steps and whispered across the tiles of the front hall. In a few seconds, she'd be opening the door and letting him into our house!

With a burst of energy I didn't know I had, I flew downstairs and grabbed her from behind just as her hand reached for the knob. The two of us got tangled up and landed in a heap in the vestibule.

She stared at me. "What's the matter with you?"

"Shhh!" I rasped. "That guy out there has been stalking me!"

Her eyes widened. "*Stalking* you?"

"Ever since the car wash," I whispered. "I've been seeing him all over town. And that black SUV has been cruising the neighborhood."

The doorbell rang again, and we both fell silent. We sat there, scarcely daring to breathe until we heard his footsteps on the walk. A moment later, the SUV roared to life and drove off.

I ran to the living room and peered outside. The coast was clear.

Melody scrambled up and stared at me. "Why would that guy stalk you? Why would anybody?"

For about a millionth of a second, I toyed with idea of telling her the guy might be a collector who'd come to pick up my soul, which I'd bargained away for 50,000 subscribers. No—she'd think I was crazy. She *should* think I was crazy. I practically thought it myself.

So I went on the offensive. "How do I know why some nutjob does what he does? You want to chase after his car and ask him?"

I was ready for a fight, when I realized that—for once—Melody wasn't in bickering mode. She looked scared.

"This is for real?" she demanded.

"You think this is fun for me?" I shot back belligerently. "Why would I make it up?"

"Because ever since this streaming thing started, you've been getting weirder and weirder! I didn't say anything to Mom and Dad because I was waiting for you to snap out of it. But this is a deal breaker!" She took out her phone and began to dial.

I snatched it away from her. "They'll call the cops!"

"Of course they will!" she exploded. "Like you should have! That's why we have police—so there's a place to call when some shady guy starts following you!"

I held on to the phone. "You'll spoil everything. The cops will start asking questions, and pretty soon GameFox229 will be out in the open. You think Mom and Dad will be thrilled about it? No—they'll shut me down! They'll shut *us* down! You can kiss your twenty percent good-bye—and just when we're about to hit 50,000 subscribers!"

"I'm fine with that," Melody insisted. "Who needs money when there's some *criminal* out there—"

"I never said he was a criminal," I interjected.

"Who else stalks people—the tooth fairy?"

"I mean, the tooth fairy *does* sort of stalk people—in their sleep."

She wasn't buying it. "But you're not saying this guy's the tooth fairy; you're saying he's a creeper."

She had me there.

"Look, Mel, I can handle myself."

She made a face that clearly stated that she didn't think so.

"Well, I've managed to avoid him this far," I wheedled. "Maybe he'll get discouraged and go away. The whole thing's probably a misunderstanding. Do you want to flush GameFox229 down the toilet over nothing?"

She was quiet for a moment, mulling it over. Finally, she said, "I won't say anything—for now. But you have to promise that if this guy shows up again, you'll come to me and we'll tell Mom and Dad together."

So I promised. And I gave her back her phone. I didn't completely trust her—how could you ever trust someone who would give up video games? But when she didn't call the store, I figured I'd made the right choice.

Maybe I was too hard on Melody. She could be a pretty loyal sister.

In exchange for 20 percent of the profits.

CHAPTER TWENTY-THREE
PAVEL DYSAN

When I volunteered to go with Cam to the beaver habitat to pick up Elvis after school on Tuesday, I already knew it was going to be for the last time.

I was done with GameFox229. Technically, the stream had gone far beyond our wildest expectations. Cam regularly played to an audience of 300,000 or better, with more than 48,000 full, paying subscribers. The 50,000 milestone was in sight and approaching fast. None of us could have imagined so much success so quickly.

But.

It wasn't worth it. It was too much work, especially if you added in transporting Elvis every day and cleaning up his messes. Trying to keep up with the scrolling (more like spinning) comment feed was like sharing a treadmill with a herd of stampeding buffalo. It might have been fun once, but it definitely wasn't fun anymore. For sure, it wasn't worth the sacrifices.

The sacrifices: Every spare minute. Cam and I could spend four hours together and not exchange a single word of real conversation. It was all GameFox229 business.

We never laughed. We never went anywhere. We didn't have the time. I still visited Sweetness and Light, but only to stock up on gummy worms so Cam could disguise his voice. Mrs. Backward kept asking, "They moved to Australia, your friends?"

Technically, it was worse than that. The Awesome Threesome had become the Awesome No-some—or at least the Elvis Solo Act. These days, the beaver was the only living creature getting any enjoyment out of the GameFox229 experience. Ask a hundred animal behavior experts and not one of them would say that a beaver could understand video games. Tell that to Elvis. He *knew* which Geldorfian warrior insects posed the greatest danger in *Guardians*. You could tell by the way he cried out and slapped his tail in warning. It would have been impossible to fake his annoyance when Cam's character got blasted back a level or two. His shoulders slumped—and he didn't even have shoulders! And when he got *really* excited, he peed all over Cam and the couch. That was the Elvis Seal of Approval.

It had its funny side, but mostly it made our job even bigger than it needed to be. Beaver control, beaver cleanup, beaver transport, beaver secrecy. The time suck was becoming more than a hassle. I got an A-*minus* on my last book report. My score on the geometry unit test was borderline B-plus! Sure, these weren't terrible grades, but A-pluses across the board were normal for me—at least they used to be before I pledged my life to GameFox229. The irony wasn't lost on me. Cam told everybody he was failing eighth grade, but *I* was the one who was actually struggling. A month ago, I was probably the front-runner to be named valedictorian—the honor that went to the kid with the highest academic average in the school. I'd worked hard to put myself in contention for that. And now—thanks to a game stream—it was all starting to slip away.

But as much as I resented Cam for that, my heart went out to the guy. The strain on him was unimaginable. I was beginning to wonder if he even needed the Zorro mask at this point. Surely his cement-gray complexion and the giant bags under his bloodshot eyes were disguise enough. His smile was as rare as the trip to Level 13 that he couldn't seem to earn. Xavier's T-shirts all over school were the last straw. GameFox229 was seeping into even those few hours that should have been GameFox-free, surrounding us like fast-encroaching rivers of molten lava. There was just no escape.

As bad as I felt about Cam, I felt even worse that Chuck and I weren't friends anymore. Oh, sure, that wasn't GameFox229's fault. Chuck and Daphne would have ended up together regardless of whether Cam had started streaming or not. But maybe the bad feelings wouldn't have gotten so out of control if the three of us hadn't had so much on our shoulders. Throw Elvis into the mix, and suddenly poor Chuck was caught between loyalty to Daphne and loyalty to Cam. Technically, some of the blame went to me, too—I should have recognized the impossible situation Chuck was in.

But I didn't, and now it was too late. Quitting GameFox229 wouldn't undo the damage. But as the old saying went: *When you find yourself in a hole, stop digging.*

I was already putting the speech together in my mind as Cam and I got our bikes from the rack and pedaled off toward the habitat. We rode in silence. His mind was a million miles away, as he psyched himself up for the hours of streaming ahead.

We biked to the woods and headed in on foot. Just as we rounded the bend in the path, where the creek came into view, Cam grabbed me by the shoulders and yanked the two of us into the underbrush.

I opened my mouth to protest but he clamped his hand over it, stifling any sound. We both peered into the clearing. There was a man at Elvis's habitat, standing over the pond, watching the beaver swim.

"It's him," Cam barely whispered.

I understood instantly. This was the mysterious stalker Cam had been seeing around town, who had even showed up at the Boxer house. To be honest, I hadn't taken it very seriously up until now. As the pressure built on Cam, he'd been getting kind of paranoid (all this talk about selling his soul for subscribers). I suspected he was imagining things. But this guy was a perfect match for the description Cam had given—tall and thin, pale skin with a black goatee. It couldn't be a coincidence.

By unspoken agreement, we backed away—slowly, silently—until we were at a safe enough distance for us to turn and run to our bikes.

"What now?" I asked. "Chill here till the guy leaves?"

Cam's voice was shaky. "He's not leaving. He's figured out that I come for Elvis every day. He's waiting for me."

"So no GameFox?" I'd been about to tell Cam that today was my last day, but I wasn't sure I wanted to leave like this. He looked really spooked—like he'd just seen a ghost.

"No beaver," he amended. "We stream without Elvis."

"Really?" I was surprised. "Your fans won't like it."

He was adamant. "That's just the way it has to be. I'm not going anywhere near that guy." He jumped on his bike. "Anyway, people care more about Level Thirteen than about Elvis these days."

We pedaled to the Boxer house and headed for the door.

"If we run into my sister," Cam advised me, "*ixnay* on telling her who we just saw at the habitat. She's ready to call the FBI on him."

Sure enough, Melody was waiting for us in the kitchen. "Where's the beaver?" she asked.

"None of your business," Cam said briskly, heading for the basement stairs.

"We're concentrating on the gaming part this afternoon," I put in, because it seemed like a real explanation was necessary. "You know, focusing on getting to Level Thirteen."

She was surprised. "Why the sudden change?"

"What do you care?" Cam shot back. "You're the one who's always complaining about the smell. Today is stink-free."

I tossed Melody an apologetic shrug as Cam dragged me down to the basement.

I kept the news to myself that I was quitting after this session. Cam had enough on his plate already, this being GameFox229's first broadcast without Elvis. I didn't want to throw him any more than he was already thrown.

To be honest, I was pretty thrown myself by what we'd seen at the habitat. The stalker was real after all! Who was this guy and what did he want? Scariest of all, was Cam in any danger? (And what about the rest of us?)

There was no time to think about that once the stream went live. We were running a few minutes late, so GameFox229 went online before its biggest audience ever— over 400,000 followers, all of them waiting, all of them impatient. Cam didn't say anything about Elvis's absence. He just started right in gaming, mumbling his usual commentary around the gummy worms in his cheeks. I held my breath, waiting for the audience's reaction. For about thirty seconds, there was nothing. Then the message feed exploded with an onslaught of comments so intense that the scroll was just a blur:

Where's the beaver?

Why isn't he there?

Is he sick?

Is he dead?

WHO KILLED THE BEAVER? . . .

I scribbled a few down for Cam to deal with, but he shook his head, determined to bluff it through, beaverless. And as he battled the impossible Level 12, the comments gradually turned away from Elvis to the epic quest to conquer this rare version of *Guardians*.

I'd never seen messages coming in at such a frantic pace. I couldn't help thinking of all the fans at our school—Jordan or Xavier or String, clad in their T-shirts, watching on their computers. Then I multiplied that by all the schools in all the towns in all the countries in the world, until my head was spinning.

It came suddenly, unexpected. Cam let out a wheeze, and for an instant, I was afraid he was choking on a gummy worm. He gestured with his controller at the computer screen. Under the main counter, which gave the current amount of followers—407,256—was a smaller display. This was the tally of full, paying subscribers. The number stood at 50,003.

He had done it. It had started as a distant dream, and here it was, glorious reality. My feelings about the stream hadn't changed (it wasn't worth the aggravation). Yet I was blown away with admiration for Cam. You could depend on it: Whatever he did went *big*.

I reached over the couch and slapped him on the shoulder exactly where Elvis would have given him a whack with his tail. I was still quitting, but at least I could walk away knowing that Cam had achieved his goal.

According to Newton's third law of motion, for every action in nature, there is an equal and opposite reaction. What happened next proved that beyond any doubt.

A comment scrolled over the feed, one of hundreds. I probably wouldn't even have noticed it, except that this one included a tiny thumbnail photograph. Of the tens of thousands of messages that had come to GameFox229 in the months Cam had been streaming, this was the first that had ever included a picture. I scrambled to the computer to get a look at it, but by that time the crawl had carried it off screen.

I pulled out my phone, logged in, and began browsing furiously through the recent comments. When I found the thumbnail, I tapped the image to expand it to full size. What I saw very nearly stopped my heart.

It was *him*—the stalker—a selfie taken at the beaver habitat. The pale, goateed mystery man held Elvis, football style, in the crook of his arm. The beaver looked terrified (although it was technically hard to judge these things). Covering the man's long, skinny torso was a GameFox229 T-shirt.

From the heights of triumph to the depths of dread in thirty seconds flat. Action, reaction. Newton's third law.

The picture was accompanied by a four-word message: *WE NEED TO TALK!*

I really didn't want to show the picture to Cam. But how could I not? This was *his* stalker and it proved that the guy was closer to Cam than even Cam suspected. The man with the goatee knew about Cam, where he lived, and where he went to school. He knew about Elvis and he knew about GameFox229. Scariest of all, he'd connected all the dots. He knew everything. Cam couldn't hide from him. There was no hiding.

It definitely soured the celebration over hitting 50,000 subscribers. After GameFox229 logged off, Cam read the message over and over: *We need to talk.*

"Maybe *he* needs to talk," was Cam's nervous response. "I've got nothing to say to him, except maybe bug off. I'm not going anywhere near that guy."

Cam couldn't go back to streaming with Elvis now, and maybe not ever. It was crazy ironic. GameFox229 had just hit its greatest heights. How could something so successful be so doomed at the same time?

Neither of us had any idea what to do. Cam had me forward the picture to Chuck (I guess because two and a half heads were better than two). I couldn't imagine what kind of wisdom he expected from good old Chucky. Chuck didn't disappoint. We got a return text thirty seconds later: *!!!!* Chuck was a man of few words—or, in this case, none at all.

"I hate to say it, Cam, but maybe Melody's right."

He made a face. "Melody's never right."

"Be serious," I persisted. "This guy knows everything about you. You can't handle this alone. You should at least tell your parents, and maybe the police."

He dug in his heels. "That would be the end of GameFox229."

"It's probably over anyway. No more Elvis. You can't make it to Level Thirteen. How long do you think the fans are going to hang around?"

I almost told him then that today was my last day, but my mouth wouldn't form the words. He looked terrible—pale, nervous, rattled, and exhausted. You didn't kick a person when he was down (even when he was too stubborn to admit that he was down).

At school the next day, the buzz was about GameFox229. For the first time ever, it wasn't all positive. What had happened to the beaver? No one could seem to speak of any other subject. Kids gathered in small groups in their GameFox229 T-shirts, voicing their disappointment over yesterday's streaming session. They had waited hours for the beaver to make an entrance, but he never showed. No one even mentioned where he was, or why he was missing. GameFox229 was a partnership, not a solo act. You couldn't just change everything in mid-stream. What was this guy trying to pull? It wasn't really GameFox229 anymore with the beaver missing. It might as well have been GameFox228 or 230.

"I don't get what all the fuss is about," Daphne complained to Chuck in the cafeteria line at lunch. "Why is it such a big deal that the beaver wasn't there?"

I was a couple of places behind them. I shot Chuck a sharp glance. Any conversation with Daphne that mentioned beavers was straying into dangerous territory.

"We can't control what some random guy on the Internet does," Chuck said quickly.

"The P.A.G. sold all those shirts," his girlfriend reminded him. "It's a bad reflection on the club if GameFox229 lets his fans down. I'm just trying to understand how the beaver fits in. A beaver can't *game*, after all—"

Casually, I reached ahead with my tray and prodded Chuck in the ribs—a gentle reminder to be careful how he answered.

He didn't. Instead, he pulled out his phone and began studiously checking messages, pretending he hadn't heard.

Daphne wouldn't let it drop. "Seriously, what's a beaver got to do with a game stream anyway?"

Chuck was getting nervous. "Nothing. How should I know?" He set his phone down on the tray so he could carry his lunch to a table. As he did, his thumb accidentally swiped the screen, bringing up the next message in the queue.

I thought my eyes would pop out of their sockets. It was the *WE NEED TO TALK!* photo—Cam's stalker holding Elvis at the habitat.

I leaped forward to flip the phone facedown, but it was already too late.

"*That's* the beaver?" Daphne shrieked. She snatched up the phone and stared at the screen. "That's Elvis! I'd know him anywhere. And that's his habitat! Who's holding him?"

Chuck seemed to shrink inside himself like a cornered animal, his eyes wide and staring. I felt a stab of fear as I realized that once he started spilling the beans, he was going to spill all of them. This whole mess was so interconnected that one tiny pebble would start an avalanche. The stalker . . . Elvis . . . GameFox229 . . . Cam.

When Chuck finally found his voice, it was squeaky and an octave higher than usual. "Daphne," he announced, "I'm breaking up with you!"

She recoiled in shock. *"What?"*

"I'm sorry," he told her, "but that's just the way it has to be." He grabbed back his phone and strode stiffly out of the lunchroom.

Daphne's burning gaze fell on me. "Pavel, what's going on?"

What was going on? I was supposed to be the smart one, but even I was having trouble processing it. Ever since he'd started with Duckne, I'd accused Chuck of being a lousy friend. I'd blamed him for everything that had happened to the Awesome Threesome just because he was the first of us to get a girlfriend. And now he had acted like the best friend in the history of friendship. He had done the only thing he could think of to change the subject under extreme pressure. And in the process, he had thrown away a relationship that meant a lot to him because there was no way he could answer without betraying Cam. He had (technically) abandoned ship to protect a friend.

"It's a long story. I'll explain later!" I slid my lunch into the garbage and ran off after Chuck.

GameFox229 was falling apart, there was a mysterious stalker after Cam, and for all we knew, every kid in town was in danger. But at least there was hope for the Awesome Threesome.

CHAPTER TWENTY-FOUR
CHUCK KINSEY

When Pavel caught up with me in the hall, he threw his arms around me and hugged me like a long-lost brother.

I wanted to punch him.

"I hope you're satisfied!" I rasped. "You've been trying to break up Duckne since day one! Well, congratulations—it's over."

At least he didn't deny it. He had the decency to look ashamed. "You were amazing back there, Chuck," he told me. "It was the only way you could have avoided blowing this whole thing sky-high. I'm not sure I would have thought of it."

"It was only amazing because you weren't the one who had to do it!"

"It was genius," he insisted.

I was still mad, but it did lessen the pain of losing Daphne. When a guy like Pavel—who really was a genius—said you were a genius, it had to feel good. Even when you just deep-sixed the best thing that ever happened to you.

"Why did you guys have to send me that stupid picture?" I complained.

"You're a part of this, too. That guy's closing in on

Cam, and Cam's too stubborn to go to his parents for help. Who knows how much trouble he could be in? We don't know who that man is, or what he wants with Cam. If today proved one thing, it's that we're still the Awesome Threesome, no matter how much we fight. We're all in this together."

Well, how could I argue with that? As heartbroken as I felt, it was definitely good to be friends with Pavel again. To be honest, I never really understood why that stopped.

But as we parted ways to head to sixth period, it was as if this huge weight descended on me. I wasn't a boyfriend anymore. My footsteps were the footsteps of a single man. This was a single man's locker. That was a single man's social studies book. The corner was chewed up, probably by somebody's dog. It had been like that when I'd gotten it at the beginning of the year. But right now it felt like it was because I didn't deserve anything perfect and new.

I wasn't in a ship anymore.

I had to find her, to apologize, to set things right. I couldn't explain the picture, but maybe if I told her how sorry I was, she'd understand. I ran to her locker, but I was too late. She must have already gone to sixth period. I suffered through the longest social studies class ever. I couldn't concentrate. The mangled corner of my textbook throbbed like an open wound in my soul.

I cut out early and stood by her locker for the entire

class change. She never showed. What was going on? Where was Daphne? I sprinted to her seventh-period class—Spanish. Kids were filing in and taking their seats. Daphne was nowhere to be seen.

Señora Goldberg looked me up and down. "You're not one of my students."

"I just need to—I'm looking for—I have to talk to—"

"Adios, amigo." She closed the door in my face.

There I stood in the hall, mind whirling, when String showed up for Spanish his usual three minutes late. "Yo, Chuck, what's good?"

"Nothing's good," I mourned. "I'm looking for Daphne, and I can't find her *anywhere*."

"That's an easy one." His shrug was a masterpiece of flexibility. Every muscle in his body moved. "She dipped."

"Dipped? You mean she *left*?"

"After fifth period," he supplied. "Seemed pretty upset, too."

"It's all my fault," I confessed. "We broke up at lunch. I just dumped her without any warning. I was a jerk—"

"Nah, that's not it. She was talking about Elvis. Kept babbling about how he could be in danger or something."

He slipped into the classroom, leaving me shaking in my sneakers. Elvis! Of course Daphne would be anxious about him after seeing that picture! Why didn't I know that? Not only was I dumb enough to throw away our ship, I was also selfish enough to think *that* was the only reason she was upset.

She must have gone to the habitat to check on Elvis!

I turned to ice. The stalker—he knew about the habitat. He'd been there at least once. He could be there *now*, lying in wait for Cam.

Daphne could be walking into a trap!

I barreled down the stairs, not bothering to stop at my locker to pick up my jacket. I hit the front door running . . . and smashed right into Mr. Fanshaw.

"Excuse me—!" When he recognized me, the guidance counselor's face twisted into a deep scowl. He was still sore from the time he caught me pulling down that GameFox229 poster from the Hallway of Heroes.

"I gotta go, Mr. Fanshaw! I'm late for my . . ." And then I drew a total blank on what I could be late for.

He had time to fold his arms in front of him while I racked my brain. ". . . my . . . my mountaineering lesson," I blurted at last.

"Don't be ridiculous."

"Come on, Mr. Fanshaw, it's an emergency!"

"No one leaves early without a signed parental excuse," he said firmly. "And certainly not today. Eighth period is the assembly where we announce all this year's class award winners. For all you know, you've won something." He thought about this for a moment and added, "Well, I don't want to get your hopes up. But you're going to be there to cheer on your classmates."

I was so torn up that I almost told him about Daphne. But that would get her in trouble for ditching. And if it turned out she *didn't* need rescuing, it would be my fault for ratting on her. She was probably ticked off enough at me already.

So, as worried as I was about Daphne, I kept my mouth shut and followed Mr. Fanshaw to his office. He wrote me up for trying to leave early—another week of detention—and made me sit on the bench until it was time for the assembly.

I kept peering through the doorway at the passing parade of students in the hall heading for the gym. I was hoping against hope to catch a glimpse of my ex-girlfriend—oh, I hated the sound of that—back from the habitat, safe and sound. No luck.

Finally, Mr. Fanshaw glanced up from some paperwork and noticed the clock. "Let's go to the gym. The assembly's about to start."

So I couldn't even sneak out then, because he was with me all the way. By the time we got to the gym, the bleachers were full. Desperately, I searched for Daphne, but she was still AWOL. I noticed Pavel and Cam sitting together near the back, and started toward them. But Mr. Fanshaw froze me with a paralyzing glare and pointed to the front row. So I was in exile, too.

This was a special assembly for eighth graders only. Part of the ceremony was announcing a bunch of awards for the athletes and the smart people, etc. None of that was me, especially the smart part, and I wasn't on any teams. The only thing I was part of was the Positive Action Group, but so was everybody else. The school would go broke if they had to give a trophy to every single pagger.

Dr. LaPierre started off by telling us that the winners announced today represented our best and brightest, but it was all our jobs to be ambassadors for the great tradition of Sycamore Middle School. P.S. Gag me.

The really pointless part was that no actual awards were being handed out at the assembly. This was just fair warning of what you were going to get—or not get, if you were getting nothing, like me.

There weren't a lot of surprises. The same kid won the math and also the science prize, which was probably a blow to Pavel, who must have been runner-up for both. Felicia Hochuli won in English, and Kelly Hannity took social studies. Athlete of the year went to String, who was his usual modest self, shaking the principal's hand and bellowing, *"How does my dust taste, losers?"* into the microphone. The art award went to Xavier, who got the biggest cheer of the day.

Pavel finally made it to the stage when they introduced the honor roll. I stomped my feet on the bleachers, happy that our friendship was back on track. I caught a hint of movement out of the corner of my eye, and turned in time to see Daphne hurry into the gym and take a seat at the edge of the third row. I felt a surge of relief, which disappeared when she shot me a look that would have melted titanium. Okay, I deserved that. But I was still really happy that she was out of danger. Her face was red, and she was breathing heavy—it was a mile and a half to the habitat, which was why Cam, Pavel, and I always biked there. Carefully, she set down a canvas shopping bag between her sneakers, which were a little muddy from the trek through the woods.

"And now we come to the award you've all been waiting for," Dr. LaPierre announced as the last of the honor rollers headed back to their seats. "Valedictorian. This honor goes to the student with the highest academic average at Sycamore Middle School—someone who exemplifies excellence and hard work. This young person's remarkable achievement shines like a beacon for all of us to follow."

I tried to catch Daphne's eye, but she ignored me, gazing straight ahead, still as a statue. My brow furrowed. The only movement seemed to be coming from the fabric of the canvas bag at her feet. Huh?

The principal's strident voice rang out in the gym. "This year's valedictorian is—Cameron Boxer!"

CHAPTER TWENTY-FIVE
CAMERON BOXER

These assemblies were always so boring that I must have been half asleep when I heard my name.

"I'm awake!" I blurted, shaking myself like a wet dog. I turned to Pavel. "Did somebody just call me?"

Pavel looked stunned. "You bet," he said, indicating the dais, where Dr. LaPierre was peering out over the rows of students. "You're the valedictorian."

"Very funny," I shot back. "Seriously, what's going on?"

"Where's our valedictorian?" the principal was announcing. "Where's Cameron?"

My first thought was: *It's a mistake.* It had to be! Nobody in their right mind would make me valedictorian. The valedictorian was some Einstein who got straight A's in everything, including fire drills—

And then my grades marched across the edge of my vision like a TV crawl: *100%... excellent job... 4.0... marvelous insight... A... A... A...*

I was getting my assignments done by the smartest kids in the whole school! None of it was my own work—*but the teachers didn't know that!*

I was the valedictorian!

My first instinct was to crawl under the bleachers, jump to the gym floor, and make a bolt for the exit. But Pavel hauled me to my feet and gave me a shove that sent me stumbling on rubbery legs down the steps in the direction of Dr. LaPierre.

The teachers were applauding, but there was dead silence from the entire eighth grade. You could have heard a pin drop on the bleachers. Dr. LaPierre was raving about the incredible transformation of my grade point average. The kids were all staring at me like I'd sprouted a second head.

I joined the principal onstage and shook his hand. I didn't say a word. I was numb. A murmur began to rise from the bleachers. Not shock or even confusion. This was anger, pure and hostile.

What did I do? I pleaded silently. *It isn't my fault I'm valedictorian!*

I gazed out over the crowd. Kelly was glaring at me—Kelly, who had started it off with her Who's Who in the American Revolution. There was Jordan, looking daggers at me. He had so much to do with my 96.7 math average. Felicia. Joe Ryerson—J.J., whatever his name was. Xavier, who saved my skin in art. The last thing I needed was to have Xavier mad at me. But no—he just seemed disappointed. He'd believed in me, and I'd let him down. It was even worse than anger.

You did this! I wanted to scream at everybody. *I never asked you to send me those assignments!*

But I was guilty. I'd spread the word that I was failing. I only did it to get out of my P.A.G. duties. But when all that free work showed up, I used it anyway. And I definitely didn't tell people to stop sending it—not even when I was getting multiple versions of every assignment.

No wonder they were mad. They thought they were helping a poor, struggling student. They did it because they liked me and they wanted to thank me for my work on the P.A.G. And Dr. LaPierre had just dynamited the myth of how much I needed their help. I was flying high academically—higher, in fact, than everybody else. I was the top student in the whole grade.

I should have known. I had math whizzes doing my algebra, top writers writing my papers, ace researchers feeding me social studies, and *chicos muy inteligentes* covering Spanish. I had Xavier fixing my art projects. What did I expect? It was like the crème de la crème in every subject coming together in a single kid. I'd created a superstudent.

I'd created the valedictorian.

All I'd wanted was to be left alone so I could do my streaming, and instead the opposite had happened. I was the total center of attention. And not just attention. Everybody hated my guts. And they had a right to.

I was a famous streamer with 50,000 paying subscribers.

At that moment, I would have traded them for a transporter so I could beam myself to Geldorf, where battling giant insects would be the biggest of my problems.

The torture didn't end quickly. Dr. LaPierre put his arm around my shoulders and went on and on about how great I was. Every compliment was another twist of the knife. The murmur from the bleachers got louder and even more unfriendly. I honestly thought I might pass out, when finally something halfway decent happened: The bell rang.

The assembly broke up, and I broke up ahead of it, running for my life.

Chuck was jogging through the crowd to intercept me. "Cam, can I talk to you for a—"

"Not now!" I cut him off. Angry faces swarmed everywhere. All that mattered was escape.

Once in the halls, I felt slightly more comfortable. Sixth and seventh graders were at their lockers, gathering their things for dismissal. They hadn't heard yet what a worthless human being I was. I even caught a few smiles as I threaded my way along the crowded corridor, hurdling backpacks.

It didn't last. Eighth graders began appearing around me, pushing through the crowd. Snippets of their conversations rose above the general hubbub:

"*You* helped him? *I* helped him! I emailed him a whole book report!"

"He told me he might not graduate!"

"I wrote that paper *twice*—once for me and once for him!"

"He said he had no studying time because of the P.A.G.!"

"He was supposed to be flunking, not valedictorian!"

"He's worse than slime!"

"Hey—there he is!"

I darted around the corner, only to run headlong into String. "Quick!" I panted. "You've got to get me out of here."

The football star's face radiated deep pain. "The String looked up to you, man. I don't look up to just anybody. And you turned out to be just another jerk."

I could have talked to him, tried to explain. But I didn't have the words. I wasn't sure there were any. I ducked under his arm and sprinted for the nearest door—only Xavier was standing there. I definitely didn't want to tangle with him at a time like this.

I wheeled around, my panic rising. The gym had totally emptied out by now. Eighth graders were everywhere, and I was Public Enemy Number One.

I had exhausted Plans A through Y, but there was still Plan Z—the custodians' exit, which was also the main loading bay for shipments coming to the school. I'd never used it before—I'd been saving it for a real emergency, like when Mr. Fan-blah-blah wanted to talk to me. This counted 1,000 percent.

As I made for the custodians' office, I became aware of a clamor in the hall behind me. A quick glance over my shoulder confirmed my worst fears. Kids were *following* me. Not chasing me exactly, but keeping pace, matching me step for step. I ducked into the deserted office—the custodians were all helping with the buses at the end of the day—and ran through to the loading dock. A red button hung from the ceiling on a cable. I pressed it and the segmented door began to lift. Nothing had ever seemed slower than the metal gate as it rose, inch by rumbling inch, from the floor.

Ticked-off eighth graders poured into the loading bay behind me—Jordan, Kelly, Felicia, J.J., String, Xavier. They kept coming. Daphne was there—she'd only become acting P.A.G. president because of my bogus flunking story. I saw Pavel and Chuck, too. If there was any chance I might survive this, it would have to be with their help. But what could the three of us do against the entire enraged eighth grade?

I dropped to the floor, rolled under the rising door, crossed the platform, and jumped down, lucky not to break both ankles. I was in a corner of the parking lot, where delivery trucks backed up to be unloaded. To my left, the pavement gave way to the schoolyard and freedom. I'd still have to face the music tomorrow. But hopefully everybody would have had a chance to cool down by then.

I ran for the playground . . . and stopped in my tracks.

A tall, thin figure stood between me and escape. Pale skin, black hair, goatee.

The stalker.

I turned on a dime and headed back toward the school. But the angry mob was still advancing on me. Talk about being caught between a rock and a hard place! I backpedaled, hands raised protectively, as if my palms could hold off the entire eighth grade. I heard a gurgling sound as my heel slipped in a muddy patch. Frantically, I twisted my body in an attempt to maintain balance. But down I went, nose-first into a huge puddle of muck.

I managed to get to my knees, slime running down my face. The mob gathered around, encircling me. I was trapped like a rat.

There was a shriek that sounded like a crying baby. I'd heard it many times before. Elvis burst out of Daphne's canvas bag and made a beeline for me, scrambling up on my shoulder and whacking me with his flat tail. If I spoke beaver, I would have said, *I get it, dude. There's danger.*

"Listen—" I wheezed. I was trying to gather my breath to warn them about the stalker, who was right behind us.

But I never got the words out, because at that moment, a voice from the middle of the throng exclaimed:

"Hey—that's GameFox229!"

My eyes widened in horror, and a trickle of mud leaked in, stinging painfully. Reality struck—I was wearing a mask of slop where my Zorro mask would be. I had a beaver on my shoulder . . .

My secret was out in the open.

Fingers pointed. Expressions of shocked recognition bloomed.

"Cam is GameFox229!"

"And the beaver—is that Elvis?"

"He was supposed to be studying, not streaming!"

"Yeah, but *we* were studying for him!"

"He got famous while we slaved!"

"That *jerk*!"

Secrets were like dominoes. Once they started to fall, they knocked each other down, until you were totally exposed.

Daphne was sputtering with rage. "We trusted you. We believed you. I took over the P.A.G. so you could bring up your stupid grades. And all the while, you were turning yourself into an Internet celebrity!"

Chuck stepped forward. "Daph—"

Her eyes shot sparks. "Shut up, Chucky! You don't

have the right to say anything else for the rest of your life! You *knew* what he was doing—don't you dare tell me you didn't! You pretended to care about Elvis while all the time you were helping this—this *horrible person* exploit him!" She wheeled on Pavel. "And you were in on it, too! You're disgusting!"

The eighth grade was seething. They already felt I'd duped them into doing my schoolwork. Now they knew why—I had become a world-famous streamer, courtesy of their hard labor. No wonder they were mad. I would have been mad, too. The mob advanced a step, blocking out the sun. Things were going to get ugly, and I only had myself to blame.

And then the stalker pushed through the crowd, staring down at me over that jet-black goatee. He reached out and locked my wrist in a powerful grip, and it scared the heck out of me. Even though I knew it was impossible, I actually waited to feel my soul being torn out of my body. Instead, he hauled me to my feet. I pulled away in fear, but he held on tight, examining the mud on my sleeve.

"That is going to stain," he told me.

Elvis gave him a warning tail-whack that must have stung.

"What do you want with me?" I rasped.

"You are GameFox229," he said with a slight accent.

I stared at him. "You've been stalking me all this time because of my *stream*?"

"Stalking?" he repeated. "No. I have followed with interest your attempts to unlock Level Thirteen. You are failing."

"I'll get there," I retorted, a little less scared, and kind of annoyed. Who was this guy to criticize my gaming?

"It is difficult," he told me. "I know this better than you. Years did I try; years did I fail. Allow me to introduce myself. My name is Draja Dubrovnik."

Pavel burst forward. "No way! You can't be Draja Dubrovnik! Draja Dubrovnik weighs four hundred pounds!"

The stalker looked embarrassed. "There are many Doritos on the path to Level Thirteen. Snacking eases the frustration."

"It's gummy worms for me," I put in.

"The weight fell off as soon as I gave up the quest," the legendary gamer went on. "But when I saw your stream, the fire was reborn in me. I thought, *I must find this boy, this GameFox229, and help him make history.*"

In spite of everything that had happened, I was energized. Not only was I not in danger, but the guy I dreaded as a stalker was really my hero. And he wanted to work with me!

Dizzy with joy and relief, I took a wobbly step.

Wrong—I was just plain dizzy. It was all catching up to me—the headaches, the fever, the lack of sleep, the pressure of the past weeks, the craziness of the assembly and everything that had come after it.

I felt myself falling, but before I actually hit the mud puddle again, everything went black.

CHAPTER TWENTY-SIX
MELODY BOXER

I was walking along the sidewalk after school when someone grabbed my shoulder and spun me around. It was Katrina, pink-faced and out of breath.

"Where are you going?"

"Home," I replied. "Where else?"

"Not the hospital?" she demanded.

I frowned. "Did I catch some terrible disease and I'm the last to know?"

"Cam collapsed on the playground after the eighth-grade assembly," she said tragically. "Nurse Kamala drove him to the emergency room."

I whipped out my phone and called Mom. It was true! She and Dad had left the store and were at the hospital with Cam!

"Don't panic, Mel. He's okay. He's resting comfortably and they've got him hooked up to an IV to pump some fluids into him, because he's badly dehydrated. He has a low-grade fever, which explains his headaches. And he says he's been really stressed and hasn't been sleeping well. Have you noticed anything different about him?"

I almost said: *Other than the fact that he's totally lost his mind?* But I didn't, because I felt really guilty. I'd known Cam had been run-down for weeks. At first, I didn't care. It served him right for always being up to his neck in some scheme. And later, when I started to worry about him, he swore me to secrecy. I should have spoken up sooner. If my brother was in the hospital, part of it was my fault.

"What do the doctors say?" I asked anxiously.

"They're doing tests now," she told me. "We should know more in a little while."

Dad picked me up and brought me to the hospital. When I saw Cam lying there with a tube in his arm, I almost cried. He didn't look any worse than usual—which, lately, wasn't that great. But his phone was just sitting there on the nightstand, and he didn't even try to play a game on it, even though the test results took a long time. Plus he thanked me for coming, which really wasn't like him.

It seemed like forever when a white-coated doctor finally came into the room, holding a computer printout. "Leptospirosis," she announced.

My father looked scared. "How bad is it?"

"Easily treatable, nothing to worry about," the woman assured us. "It's a bacterial infection caused by human contact with animals, notably rodents. Mice, rats . . ."

Mom was alarmed. "We have nothing like that."

"Perhaps squirrels or chipmunks," the doctor went on.

Mom shook her head. "Outside, maybe, but they keep their distance."

"How about pets? Guinea pigs? Hamsters?"

"Beavers?" I blurted suddenly.

If looks could kill, the one I got from Cam would have taken me out on the spot.

"Well, I suppose," the doctor mused. "But I can't imagine where Cameron could interact with a beaver around here. It would have to be very close contact."

I pictured Elvis crawling all over Cam during those streaming sessions—in his lap; on his shoulder; wrapped around him like a scarf; even sitting on his head, pummeling Cam with his flat tail.

I spilled my guts about GameFox229—the secret streaming in the basement, the beaver's role, the legions of followers, the 50,000 subscribers. As I went on, our parents' eyes got wider and wider, until Mom and Dad looked like manga characters.

Until this point, they'd been very gentle toward their ailing son. But this latest development—along with the good news that his leptospirosis was curable—brought the worry level down and the anger level up.

"Cam, how could you do all this and not tell us?" Mom demanded.

"You would have said no," he explained reasonably.

"Of course we would have said no!" Dad raved. "*No* was invented for people like you! Don't you think we should be told when there's a mysterious stranger following you around town?"

"That was just a misunderstanding," Cam supplied. "It wasn't a stranger. It was Draja Dubrovnik."

I snapped alert. "Draja Dubrovnik the *gamer*? What did he want with you?"

Cam looked sheepishly pleased. "He's a GameFox229 fan. He wants another shot at Level Thirteen."

Mom and Dad were speechless. How had their son become an Internet celebrity without them having the slightest inkling it was even happening?

The doctor addressed Cam. "I'm going to keep you overnight to start you on the antibiotic. And I'll have to report this beaver to the health department. Animal control will pick him up."

I stared at her. "You're going to kill Elvis?"

She smiled tolerantly. "I'm no rodent expert, but a similar antibiotic should cure your furry friend. If Cameron got it from him, he has the infection, too."

"Daphne was right," Cam said in amazement. "No wonder Elvis was losing weight. He has lepto—you know, *that*."

"A trip to the vet will straighten him out," the doctor confirmed.

"They can do anything they like with him," Mom said firmly, "so long as he stays out of *our* house." She turned on my brother. "And I haven't decided yet how I feel about *you.*"

Cam was released from the hospital the next morning. Mom and Dad kept him home from school for a few days, while the medicine knocked out his leptospirosis. That was probably a good thing. The entire eighth grade was mad enough to murder him.

The whole business had come into the open at the eighth-grade assembly. Cam had so many academic stars doing his work for him that he ended up valedictorian. That was news to the academic stars who thought he was failing—mostly because he said he was. Not only that, but the news got out that he was GameFox229, too, which was the last straw. In other words, they had done double schoolwork so he could become a streaming star. Jack the Ripper was more popular around school than my brother.

The trash cans were all stuffed with GameFox229 T-shirts, most of them ripped up, scissored, or even burned. Some had messages scribbled on them with magic marker.

CHEAT one of them said. *DIRTBAG* blazoned another. *YOU STINK. SLIMEBALL.* It just got nastier from there.

The sixth and seventh graders were mad at Cam, too, although none of us had been doing his assignments. The whole thing was worse because he'd been so admired before as the founder of the P.A.G. It was hard to accept when someone you looked up to turned out to be someone you should have been looking down on. Of course I understood Cam had never deserved all that credit for starting the P.A.G. in the first place, but there was no way I'd ever convince anyone of that now.

Luckily, there was no guilt by association. Nobody blamed me. It even earned me sympathy from some people: How did it feel to be the sister of the worst kid in the world? Katrina kept asking me if I needed a shoulder to cry on. It was getting kind of annoying.

Cam knew all this was going on—he was getting updates from Pavel and Chuck. They were loyal to a point, but neither was willing to speak up for Cam at school. It just wasn't done. He was poison, and if you liked him, you could be poison, too. The only other person who called Cam was Draja Dubrovnik. They were friends now—go figure. They could talk about Level 13 for hours.

Sigh.

I used to be jealous of Cam, because everything went his way. No matter how badly he messed up, he always came out smelling like a rose. But in this case, he had run into a brick wall. You couldn't forgive a guy who lied to you, used you, and became a streaming celebrity *and* valedictorian off your hard labor.

So now I should have been happy because fate had finally caught up with my brother and he was getting what was coming to him. But believe it or not, I felt sorry for him, because he was totally destroyed.

He sensed it, too. He was moping around the house, not gaming, or even looking online to see if his GameFox229 followers were clamoring for his return. (I checked. They were. Cam and Draja Dubrovnik weren't the only two gamers obsessed with Level 13.)

I think Cam was happy to stay away from school as long as possible. Funny—a normal person would know he had to go back eventually. Not Cam. He could lock it away indefinitely and live in the moment.

It happened on day six. Mom and Dad had already decided that Cam would go back to school the next morning. I was terrified at the prospect of Cam facing the students of Sycamore. It was going to be awful. My brother had run out of miracles, and the clock was ticking.

There was a letter in the mail from Andromeda Web Enterprises.

"Those are the guys who run the streaming service," said Cam.

"They're probably wondering what happened to GameFox229," I mused.

He tore open the envelope. "It's a check—my subscriber money. I wonder how much—"

And then his jaw dropped open like the digger of a power shovel, and he gawked in amazement.

CHAPTER TWENTY-SEVEN
DAPHNE LEIBOWITZ

We were such idiots!

How could we have been so wrong about Cameron Boxer? The whole school was in open revolt because we'd thought he'd taken advantage of us and used us to make himself famous.

But all this time he'd been doing it for the P.A.G.

That's what GameFox229 had been from the very start—a secret fund-raiser. While I messed around with piddling little ideas like a car wash or a T-shirt sale, Cam had been building up his stream to earn big money for the Sycamore Library. And when he came back to school after getting better from leptospirosis, he turned over all his streaming profits—$186,274—to the P.A.G. It put the library building fund over the top, and construction was slated to begin this summer.

It had to be the greatest show of student leadership in history. He spearheaded a giant stealth fund-raising campaign. And even though we didn't know it was happening, he found a way to allow us all to participate by doing his homework and being GameFox229 fans. Even when we all hated him, he didn't say a word in his own defense. He didn't want to spoil the surprise when he signed over that ginormous check to the P.A.G. What a moment! I thought Mr. Fanshaw was going to spontaneously combust. Dr. LaPierre got right on the PA system and told everybody how grateful we should be to Cam. The principal never figured out that his valedictorian's sky-high GPA was just another piece of Cam's grand strategy.

Let's just say that a lot of kids felt pretty stupid about throwing out their GameFox229 T-shirts.

Cam was so awesome that it made me a little bit sad because I could never be a student leader on his level. No one could. I might run the P.A.G. for a while, but it took someone like Cam to create it and make it great. My ideas might raise a little money, but I would never have the vision to start a secret game stream. And I definitely wouldn't have been able to take it big time, even if it meant getting leptospirosis in the process. He sacrificed his health for the P.A.G.

Dr. Casper said that Cam couldn't have predicted the leptospirosis part, because most beavers didn't have it. The veterinarian said it probably came from an infected squirrel or field mouse going to the bathroom in the stream next to Elvis's habitat. Yuck. Not even Cam Boxer could do anything to prevent that.

The good news was that Elvis had already put on a couple of ounces now that he was healthy again. Dr.

Casper hadn't weighed him yet, but I could tell. Chucky agreed with me. We were back together. Or, to be more accurate, we never really broke up in the first place. It was all part of Cam's fund-raising master plan for the P.A.G. I was coming to see that there was something really special between Chucky and Pavel and Cam. Even though a guy was in a relationship, he still needed time to hang out with his friends. It could only make Chucky a better person to be close to a great guy like Cam and someone supersmart like Pavel. In fact, Pavel was the new valedictorian. When Cam told Mr. Fanshaw he couldn't accept the position, the honor automatically went to the second-highest GPA.

I didn't approve of that. "You know, Cam, I get that you didn't *exactly* earn your grades in the usual way. But everybody understands that it was part of your fund-raising strategy. Nobody deserves to be valedictorian more than you."

Cam was adamant. "Pavel does. He's the smartest kid in Sycamore by a mile—and his grades would have been even higher if he wasn't spending all his time backing me up with the stream. Chuck, too—I was a jerk to these guys when I was GameFox229. The fact that they forgive me proves what great friends they are."

"Gummy worms for everybody!" Pavel announced magnanimously. "Let's all go to Sweetness and Light. You too, Daphne—you're one of us."

Chucky beamed all over his face.

"Good idea," Cam approved. "My treat. I owe you guys. Man, do I ever!"

As we started down Main Street toward Sweetness and Light, it hit me. That was the best Cam Boxer quality of all: his modesty. In his mind he owed us, when it was so obvious that everybody owed him.

Cam was making community service history every day with the P.A.G.—and *I* had a front-row seat. What a special time to be a student at Sycamore Middle School!

CHAPTER TWENTY-EIGHT
CAMERON BOXER

"This is so ill," I said. "It might be the illest thing that's ever happened to me."

I wasn't streaming or even gaming. I was in our kitchen with Pavel and Chuck, waiting for a very special visitor.

Melody breezed in and selected a drinkable yogurt from the fridge. "Well, what do you know?" she greeted us. "The Awful Threesome, together again. Is your playdate here yet?"

"He's not a playdate!" I exploded.

She shrugged. "Whatever. And remember—if Dad catches you streaming, you're going out to the habitat to bunk with Elvis. Now that's streaming—in a real stream."

"We're not going to stream," Pavel promised. "We're tackling one of humankind's greatest challenges."

Melody snorted. "Yeah, right." She flitted upstairs.

I'd never admit it in front of my sister, but I was happy that GameFox229 was over. I hated it. Streaming had taken my favorite thing—gaming—and turned it into a chore, a responsibility, a misery, and a source of stress and exhaustion. I wouldn't stream again for all the money in the world—which was what they actually sent me. I guess

20 percent of that belonged to Melody, but we both agreed that donating it all to the P.A.G. was the right thing to do.

That giant check turned out to be just enough to hit the fund-raising goal for the public library. Mom and Dad weren't even mad at me for giving all that cash away; Boxer's Furniture Showroom was getting the contract for every single piece of furniture for the new building. It wasn't just a win-win; it was a win-win-win-win. And the biggest win was that the kids at school seemed to think that I'd done everything for *them*. I was a hero. I wasn't even 100 percent sure how. But I'd take it.

A lot of people might call me stupid for dropping GameFox229—I was getting rich and I only would have gotten richer if I'd stuck with it. Well, maybe and maybe not. My followers wouldn't have waited for Level 13 forever. But more important, streaming had never totally been about money for me. It was about my lifestyle—being able to do what I loved for my real career. What I learned was I didn't love streaming. Eventually, I started hating it. And if I hated it, it wasn't really my lifestyle anymore.

When you were a kid, adults were always telling you stuff you were "obsessed" with. Mom and Dad said I was obsessed with video games, and I was okay with that. If gaming was an obsession, then I was thrilled to be obsessed.

Streaming was different. I *had* gotten obsessed with GameFox229. And it almost cost me everything: My school life—if it hadn't been for all the money, nobody ever would have talked to me again. My friends—nothing was worth cracking up the Awesome Threesome. And even my health.

It had been a close call, a near miss—like in a road-racing game, where just a couple of inches of pavement stood between you and total wipeout. I could have been the driver in the ditch, broken in pieces and on fire. I felt pretty lucky that it hadn't gone that way.

Chuck consulted his watch. "He's late. Do you think he's really coming?"

"The guy's an artist," Pavel reasoned. "They're entitled to be late."

Ding-dong.

I opened the door and there he was. Tall, thin. Jet-black hair and goatee. Draja Dubrovnik, skinny version.

That was why this was the illest day ever. The one and only Draja Dubrovnik was going to join me in making video game history. Side by side, we were going to take down *Guardians of Geldorf,* Level 13.

I even let him have my sweet spot on the couch, sculpted to perfection by the thousands of hours I'd spent on it.

I sat down next to him with the spare controller, "Mr. Dubrovnik, this is such an honor—"

He cut me off. "Speak not of honor. There is work to be done. Begin!"

Ding-dong. The doorbell again.

"Don't answer it," Pavel hissed.

Chuck was nervous. "What if it's the cops? We're about to see content that was banned in forty-seven states!"

We heard Melody walking across the hall to the front door. Then: "Chuck—your girlfriend's here!"

"Daphne?" Chuck was caught off guard. "She hates video games."

"You must end your entanglement immediately," Draja advised in his deep voice.

We heard Daphne on the basement stairs. "Don't start yet, you guys. Not without the most important part."

She came into view, struggling with the pet carrier. Inside, Elvis's eager face was pressed up against the bars. When he saw the game console and the TV, he practically lost it. I wasn't sure if beavers could cry—and I didn't know who to ask, not even Google. But I could have sworn the beaver had tears in his eyes.

"Daph—?" Chuck was confused. "You're okay with this? What about animal exploitation?"

Daphne hung her head, shamefaced. "I thought that before. Then I went on YouTube and watched some old clips of GameFox229. You were right. Elvis *loves* video games. It would be cruel to keep him away from something he enjoys so much."

When she opened the gate, Elvis shot out of the cage

and scrambled up the side of the couch so fast that he whacked Draja in the back of the head with his tail. Pavel, Chuck, and I were horrified at the disrespect—not that a beaver could ever understand the gaming royalty we had in our presence. This was the equivalent of punching the Queen of England, or at least soaking her with a water balloon.

But Draja was cool with it. "All gamers are welcome here," he told Elvis.

The prospect of playing alongside this video virtuoso terrified me. How could I possibly measure up? What if I suddenly became all thumbs on the controller and looked like a newbie in front of Draja?

But as the familiar graphics of *Guardians* appeared on the screen, I slipped easily into gaming mode. Along with my own character, I closely monitored my partner's, knowing that he was being manipulated by the most skilled of hands.

Elvis seemed a little taken aback by our tandem play— and probably also because I wasn't wearing my mask and mumbling through gummy worms. But he was so happy to be back in the saddle again that he got really focused.

"Look at that concentration," Daphne whispered.

"Thank you," Draja acknowledged.

"I'm talking about Elvis," she snapped. "He's totally absorbed!"

We plowed through the first eleven levels at lightning speed. I'd been playing *Guardians* every day for weeks, and Draja was—let's face it—Draja.

"This is like watching da Vinci painting the *Mona Lisa*," Pavel whispered in awe.

Once we reached 12, though, everything slowed down. I risked a sideways glance at my wingman. Draja's long fingers, which had been dancing over the controls, were suddenly heavy and clumsy, jerking awkwardly. A feeling of déjà vu came over me, like I'd been through this before. And I had—not with Draja by my side but on my own. The legendary gamer was having trouble—*just like me.*

Pavel and Chuck looked on in dismay. Draja Dubrovnik didn't stall out! He vaporized all obstacles, crushed the opposition, and pressed on to victory!

"When you tanked on Level Twelve," Chuck whispered in my ear, "was it sort of like this?"

"*Exactly* like this," I whispered back.

Elvis, too, could sense that the tide was turning against us. He got twitchy, and started making those crying-baby sounds. The warning thump of his tail against the back of the couch increased to the constant pounding of war drums.

"What's going on, Chucky?" Daphne demanded. "Why's Elvis so upset?"

We were right outside the Hive Dome, on the verge of

busting in. But every time Draja figured out a way to defeat whichever warrior insect was defending the portal, some new bug would come along and stomp us. He was walloped by weevils and routed by roaches. I struggled to his defense, only to be stabbed through the heart by a hornet with a stinger as long as a jouster's lance. Hemorrhaging life points down to the negative numbers, I was out of the battle. All I could do was watch in agony as my idol was eaten, beaten, lasered, Tasered, perforated by projectiles, blown up, and burned to a crisp. Elvis was wailing so loud that the basement reverberated like a hospital nursery. He climbed onto Draja's head, clinging to clumps of thick dark hair, rocking back and forth in agitation.

The beatdown wasn't over yet. An especially belligerent dung beetle rolled a giant poop ball over Draja, flattening him. At last, he was dismantled to his component atoms and scattered across eight million parsecs of empty space. By the time the dust cleared, he had to fight through five levels even to reach the spot I'd been blasted back to.

It would have taken the heart out of anybody. Not Draja Dubrovnik. He soldiered on like the pro he was, with me brawling along beside him. But as soon as we reached Level 12, the problems started all over again.

"Munchies, please," Draja requested, never taking his eyes from the screen.

Pavel and Chuck ran upstairs and ransacked the kitchen,

231

returning with armloads of snacks. A full pound of Doritos disappeared during a single battle with a swarm of poison-spewing dragonflies. I didn't even see the famous gamer eat them. One minute the bag was full, the next it was empty.

After about forty-five minutes, my sister came downstairs and stood behind Draja, watching the action on the screen.

"Beat it, Melody," I hissed at her. "You're not a gamer anymore, remember?"

In answer, she stepped around the couch, yanked the controller out of the exhausted Draja's hands, and sat down beside him, hip-checking him out of the sweet spot.

Pavel, Chuck, and I were horrified. Didn't she understand who this was? It was all I could do to work up the courage to *talk* to this legend, and Melody was bullying him like he was some random nobody!

"You guys are hopeless," she murmured, setting to work against the planetary defenses.

I was furious. "Do you know who you're insulting? He was a gaming star before you were even born!"

"He's hopeless, too," she retorted, jumping effortlessly over a swarm of helicopter tarantulas with a tap of the Y control.

Chuck was confused. "I thought you quit video games, Melody."

"I did," she confirmed. "But that doesn't mean I'm not still *good*."

I'd never been so mad at my sister—and that was saying something, because she could drive anybody crazy. "Melody, put down that—"

"Wait a minute!" Daphne's exclamation silenced me. "Look at Elvis!"

We all stared. Thirty seconds ago, the beaver had been reeling around the couch, the picture of misery and defeat. Now he was up again, stiff as a pointer, drinking in every move Melody made on-screen.

"Forget it, Elvis," I told him. "No way can she do what Draja can't!"

Watching her play, though, my tongue twisted inside my mouth. There was always something different about the way my sister gamed—different and special. She had skills—I couldn't deny that. Under her old gamer tag, Evil McKillPeople, she'd been a monster at *Guardians* and a lot of other games, too. But it was more than that. She was unpredictable—it was almost impossible to follow what she was doing and anticipate what was coming next. When most gamers were just responding to what was right in front of them, she was thinking three or four moves ahead.

"To do the same thing over and over again and expect a different result," she lectured, fingers just a blur, "is the definition of insanity."

"But what choice is there?" Draja reasoned. "The game is one of battle. Fighting is the only option."

"You're fighting the enemy like they're human," she replied. "They're not. They're bugs. They have a hive mentality. Defeat one and hundreds more take its place. But trick one and you've tricked them all."

"Oh, that's great!" I exploded sarcastically. "Trick them—no problem! What are you going to do—pull a quarter out of their segmented butts—?"

Draja held up a hand to silence me. "Proceed," he told Melody respectfully.

Calm amid the blizzard of insect firepower that boiled all around her character, Melody pressed down the B control to bring up the menu of special powers at her disposal. But instead of choosing *nuke* or *laser* or *meteor shower* or even *cyber-weapon*, she opted for *molecular transformation*. She aimed her sights on a distant hillside, and selected *sugar* from the pop-up menu. With a rumble, the distant mountain morphed into a vast heap of sugar crystals.

I threw down my own controller, dropping my character out of play. "Mel, that has to be the dumbest—"

The mosquitoes were first. Instead of attacking Melody, they took off for the mountain like a squadron of F-16s. The ants went next, not as fast, but much greater in number, swarming over the planetary surface like a massive dark wave. They all followed—flying, crawling, hopping, gliding, inching, darting, scrambling. From the tiniest no-see-um to the tallest of the towering stick insects, the defenders of Geldorf made for Mount Sugar in a rustling, buzzing, chirping, screeching parade that raised the dust from the alien landscape. And there it was, the Hive Dome, completely unprotected, not a stinkbug in sight.

Melody didn't even have to blast through the titanium of the dome. The Grand Portal was wide open, the throne empty. The scepter lay abandoned on the floor. The Geldorfian president had removed it from his thorax so it wouldn't slow him down in the race to Mount Sugar. The six of us—Pavel, Chuck, Daphne, me, Draja, and Elvis— gazed in wonder as Melody's character entered the throne room and picked up the scepter.

The scene faded to pixels and a message appeared:

LEVEL 12 COMPLETE
BEGIN LEVEL 13? Y/N

The room was as still as an empty tomb. Elvis was filled with such joy that he went suddenly boneless, causing him to ooze over the back of the couch and flop to the floor. He lay there, stunned, for only a second before scrambling back up again. The beaver was no dummy. He didn't want to miss a second of this.

Draja got down on one knee in front of my sister and

kissed her hand like she was some kind of princess. I lost a lot of respect for him that day. But I had to admit that almost nobody in the world could have managed what she just had. Melody—who didn't even like video games anymore—had accomplished Mission Impossible.

She looked pleased. "What do you say, guys? Ready for Level Thirteen?"

"Hit it!" Chuck exclaimed.

Elvis squeaked in agreement.

Melody handed the controller back to Draja. "You do it. You're the legend."

Then Draja Dubrovnik—the most celebrated name in the history of gaming—turned to me. "The privilege should go to GameFox229."

And the next thing I knew, the device was in my hands. My entire body trembled as I pressed A to begin the next level.

The controller began to shake wildly as the spaceship was sucked into a wormhole and blasted clear across the galaxy. The screen lit up with kaleidoscopes of color in impossible fractals and zigzags.

"Cam—do something!" Pavel urged.

"Do what?" I yelled back. My ship was careering out of control, so evasive action wasn't an option. There were no enemies to fire at. Desperately, I swiveled the joystick around the screen, but no drop-down menu appeared to offer a way out. I squeezed the controller with all my might, hanging on for dear life. If it vibrated out of my grasp in front of Draja, I wasn't sure I could survive the humiliation.

And just as suddenly, it was over, and we were approaching our destination—a tiny blue disc against the blackness of space.

Chuck pointed. "Isn't that—?"

"Earth," Pavel supplied.

"Fascinating," Draja breathed. "After the conquest of Geldorf, the human fleet returns home."

Elvis leaned forward and peered at the TV like a near-sighted old lady.

"That's right, Elvis," Daphne approved. "That's where you live."

As if a beaver could recognize planet Earth from the NASA photographs.

The controller was behaving now, responding normally as the familiar sphere grew closer, and I aimed the ship into the swirling clouds and we began to descend into Earth's atmosphere.

I felt an explosion of anticipation, but there was nervousness in there, too. A quick glance at Pavel and Chuck told me that my fellow Awesome Threesomers were thinking the same thing. This was epic, thrilling. The line from Star Trek—*Where no one has gone before*—played in an endless loop in my head, complete with the music. Still, it was kind of scary. We were about to witness the long-lost Level 13 that had brought hundreds of thousands of followers to my GameFox229 stream. But I couldn't help wondering about the reason Level 13 got to be so long-lost in the first place. This version of *Guardians* was banned due to "inappropriate content." What could be so awful, so unacceptable, so gross, so terrifying, so offensive, or so upsetting that millions of citizens in forty-seven states couldn't be allowed to view it?

We were about to find out.

We burst through the cloud cover and got our first view of our beloved planet. Gasps were torn from all our throats. I fumbled the controller and barely managed not to drop it. A crying lament came from deep inside Elvis.

Earth was a smoldering ruin.

We swooped low over a city of shattered buildings and blackened landscape. Thick smoke hung over everything like a pall.

"What happened?" Pavel breathed in awe.

"There can be only one explanation," Draja intoned gravely. "While we were off making war on Geldorf, another alien race came to make war on us."

"Or we made war on ourselves and wrecked our home world," Melody added in a hushed tone.

"You're lucky you're not human," Daphne told Elvis. "People stink."

"You think this is why the original *Guardians* got banned?" Chuck suggested. "Like this was too much for people to handle?"

Draja shook his head and pointed dramatically. "*There* is the reason."

As we passed low over crumbled apartment blocks, smashed churches, and the remains of what had once been stadiums and bridges, a lone billboard poked above the rubble like a weed growing through broken pavement. The sign was dented and scorched, but you could still read the message:

FOR WHITER TEETH. BRUSH WITH DAZZLE

"That's it?" I stared at my all-time hero. "Brush with Dazzle? In video games, you can blow up whole planets, wipe out entire populations, and break every law in the book! You can see brain-eating monsters, exploding body parts, and guts all over the place! What's so bad about a toothpaste ad?"

"I thought you knew," the legendary gamer told me. "They never got permission from the Dazzle Toothpaste Company. *That's* why the game was banned—for copyright infringement."

We gawked at the face that had graced so many eSports magazines. Pavel, Chuck, and I were blown away. Melody's expression radiated disbelief. Even Daphne—who knew nothing about video games and wanted to know even less—was astonished. *This* was Level 13? Brush with Dazzle? Copyright infringement?

I'd devoted myself to this stupid game! I'd almost ruined my life over it! And not just me—there were over four hundred thousand people on the Internet determined to follow me to the end of the world because I was about to unlock the great mystery for them!

Our dumbfounded silence was suddenly shattered by a high-pitched sound somewhere between a cackle and a scream. We all wheeled to see Elvis rolling on the back of the couch, holding on to his furry belly with both front paws.

"Is he"—I was thunderstruck—"*laughing?*"

"Impossible." Daphne shook her head. "Beavers can't laugh!"

Pavel looked thoughtful. "I read about an experiment where these scientists made rats giggle by tickling them. Technically, beavers are rodents, too."

"Yeah, but Elvis wasn't just giggling," Chuck pointed out. "He was cracking up."

Melody was disgusted. "Are you seriously saying that this smell factory—who can't tell the difference between our couch and a public restroom—has a sense of humor?"

The last word came from Draja. "Of course he does. He is one of us. We gamers have many unexpected talents. Watch and listen—he will show his amusement again."

But Elvis had other ideas. With an elaborate yawn, he slithered off the couch, scrambled across the floor, and stuffed himself through the open door of the pet carrier. Within seconds, he was fast asleep.

For the world's first video-gaming beaver, it was game over.

Keep reading for a look at
War Stories, by Gordon Korman

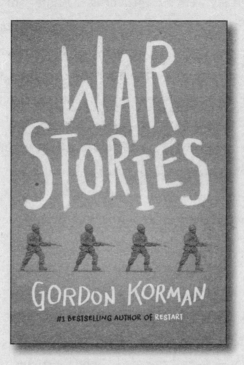

There are two things Trevor loves more than anything else: playing war-based video games and his great-grandfather Jacob, who is a true-blue, bona fide war hero. But as the two retrace the steps Jacob took during the war, Trevor discovers there's more to the story than what he's heard his whole life, causing him to wonder about his great-grandfather's heroism, the truth about the battle he fought, and the importance of genuine valor.

To hear G.G. tell it, everybody in World War II had an easy job compared with infantry soldiers, which is what he was. The navy—they were out for a cruise. Pilots—nice view from up there. Tank crews—what did they know about sore feet? Engineers—easier to build a bridge than to march across it when the dynamite goes off. Sometimes, it almost sounded like G.G. hated the war. The old man had an explanation for that too. He and his comrades in Bravo Company had been almost as skilled at complaining as they'd been at soldiering. And their favorite topic for complaining was the fact that the entire Allied Expeditionary Force, clear on up to General Eisenhower, was having a sweet time of it, while leaving all the dirty work to them.

"Come on," Trevor chided his great-grandfather. "The airborne were heroes too. They were taking enemy fire when all they could do was hang there while their parachutes came down."

"I suppose," G.G. conceded. "The Germans shot at everybody, not just us. Come to think of it, the whole war would have been a lot better without them messing it up—them and their Third Reich."

The two laughed while, in the kitchen, Trevor's father shook his head, half-amused, half-disgusted. This was the way their conversations always went—war, war, and more war. Sometimes he felt like he should put a stop to it. Trevor's interest in World War II was turning into a full-blown obsession. He played video games about it, read books, watched movies, built models. Both his rooms—at his mother's house and here too—were plastered with posters commemorating military units and major battles. Where were the sports heroes? The TV and movie stars? Was it natural for a twelve-year-old kid to be so totally engrossed in something that glorified death and destruction?

On the other hand, he was thrilled that Trevor had a real relationship with his great-grandfather. After all, what did a twelve-year-old boy have in common with a ninety-three-year-old veteran? It was a *good* thing—in a way. And the reason it worked was that World War II was all Trevor ever wanted to hear about. And Private First Class Jacob Firestone of Bravo Company had plenty to say on the subject.

"Dinner's ready." Trevor's father set the bowl of spaghetti and meatballs on the table. "One request tonight: Can we at least be done with our salads before anyone mentions the word *grenade*?"

Trevor rolled his eyes. "Dad—you're insulting G.G."

The old man took his place at the table. "Don't worry about me, Trevor. I don't insult so easy. You couldn't insult me if you—"

"Dropped a grenade in your pants?" Trevor finished.

G.G. shot him an appreciative grin. "Good one!"

Dad sat down with a sigh. "You two. Eighty-one years separating you, and you're both the same kind of idiot."

Trevor beamed. Having anything in common with his great-grandfather was okay with him—even idiocy. But he did his best to hold off on the war talk until they'd started on the spaghetti.

Spaghetti was G.G.'s favorite food, because during his deployment in Europe, it was "the only thing those slop-slingers in the kitchen couldn't turn into latrine runoff."

Trevor cackled his appreciation. That was another thing he admired about the war. Soldiers were great at cracking jokes.

His father made a face. "Can we please talk about something else?"

The old man pulled a piece of paper from his pocket and began to unfold it. "This letter came in yesterday's mail. It's from the village council of Sainte-Régine."

"Sainte-Régine?" Dad repeated.

G.G. shrugged. "Some one-horse town in France. Our unit passed through there back in forty-four."

Dad took the letter from his grandfather and scanned it. "According to this, you didn't just pass through. You fought a battle there and liberated the place!"

"What?" Trevor was up like a shot, reading over his father's shoulder. It was true. PFC Jacob Firestone of the United States Army (Retired) was the last surviving participant of the Battle of Sainte-Régine. That coming May, in commemoration of the seventy-fifth anniversary of victory in Europe, the village was holding a celebration of its liberation from German occupation. And they were inviting G.G. to be the guest of honor.

Trevor was bursting with pride. "Wow—it's like the whole town wouldn't even be there if it wasn't for you."

G.G. was modest. "I'm sure some other unit would have turned up if we'd decided to sleep in that day."

Dad set the letter down on the table. "It's a real honor. It's a shame you have to miss it."

Trevor was horrified. "Why would he miss it?"

"France isn't exactly around the corner," his father explained. "It's just not practical for a man his age to make a trip like that."

"But he *has* to go," Trevor pleaded. "He's the only guy from the battle still alive! There's nobody else left for those people to thank."

Dad tried to be patient. "Think about Grandpa. Does he ever like people to make a big fuss over him? You know he doesn't. He doesn't visit the monuments or go to the reunions. He refuses to be honored in the Memorial Day parade. He won't even look out the window when it passes by his house. Believe me, the last thing he wants to do is take a trip to France."

"But Dad—"

"If you two knuckleheads are through deciding what I want," G.G. interrupted, "maybe you'd like to hear my take on all this."

Grandson and great-grandson turned to face the old man.

"I'm going," he announced.

Trevor launched into a victory dance.

"Be reasonable," Dad urged his grandfather. "Don't you realize what a strain this trip would be on you?"

"I made it once before," the old man snapped back. "With a fifty-pound pack on my back and people shooting at me."

"You were eighteen years old!" Dad argued.

"Seventeen. I lied about my age at the recruiting center. People said they'd never take me, but I proved them wrong. Just like you're wrong now."

Daniel Firestone stood his ground. "Grandpa, I just can't let you make a trip like this alone."

His grandfather scowled at him. "Who said anything about being alone?" He grinned at Trevor. "Ever been to France?"

Trevor's jaw fell open halfway to his knees.

Great Reads
from Bestselling Author
GORDON KORMAN

How does an all-star slacker end up achieving more than any overachiever could ever imagine?

After losing his memory, it's not only a question of who Chase is–it's a question of who he was…and who he's going to be.

Can a nobody kid become somebody with the help of a seventeenth-century ghost—and right a wrong from the past?

About the Author

Gordon Korman is the #1 bestselling author of five books in The 39 Clues series as well as eight books in his Swindle series: *Swindle, Zoobreak, Framed, Showoff, Hideout, Jackpot, Unleashed,* and *Jingle*. His other books include *This Can't Be Happening at Macdonald Hall!* (published when he was fourteen); *The Toilet Paper Tigers*; *Radio Fifth Grade*; *Slacker*; *Restart*; *Whatshisface*; the trilogies The Hypnotists, Island, Everest, Dive, Kidnapped, and Titanic; and the series On the Run. He lives in New York with his family and can be found on the Web at gordonkorman.com.